Love 16

Love 16

Love, parents and other problems

Victoria Coren

C

CENTURY
London Sydney Auckland Johannesburg

First published in 1989 by Century
an Imprint of Century Hutchinson Ltd
Brookmount House, 62–65 Chandos Place,
London WC2N 4NW

Century Hutchinson Australia Pty Ltd
89–91 Albion Street, Surry Hills,
New South Wales 2010

Century Hutchinson New Zealand Ltd
PO Box 40–086, 32–34 View Road, Glenfield,
Auckland 10, New Zealand

Century Hutchinson South Africa (Pty) Ltd
PO Box 337, Bergvlei, 2012 South Africa

Phototypeset by Input Typesetting Ltd
Made and printed in Great Britain by
Mackays of Chatham

British Library Cataloguing in Publication Data

Coren, Victoria
    Love 16: love, parents and other problems.
    1.Adolescents. Interpersonal relationships
    I.Title
    305.2'35

ISBN 0–7126–3012–0

This book is dedicated to
SPGS Class of 1990
(with lots of affection)

Contents

Introduction

No-one ever reads Introductions, do they? I mean, even now, I'm meant to be a conscientious A-level English student but when I pick up a book for the first time there's no wading about through Introductions, Prefatory Notes, Historical Backgrounds, Original Preface to 1830 Editions and all that. After thirty pages of Horace McWhirter (Editor)'s interpretation of the climactic scene (p. 831) and what Graham Greene said about it, and how the writer had spent forty-seven years in debtor's prison prior to writing the book, who cannot feel totally unable to address the book itself?

So I could pretty safely assume at this juncture that I am speaking to myself alone. However, you can never be sure what may happen in a few years' time, and who is to say that I will not end up on a GCSE English syllabus? I mean nowadays they have Adrian Mole and the Beano, and people complain it's biased towards the literate pupils — not like when I were a lass, all those months ago, it was Doctor Johnson and a slap on the back of the head with a bicycle chain and like it. If I were to end up on the GCSE Eng Syll, the candidates would expect to read the Introduction and not the rest of the book, so I'd better put one in.

It's actually less of an Introduction and more of an excusatory note. I should really have got my mother to write it. You see, I never meant to write a book in the first place. I've been writing short pieces for a couple of years in the Daily Telegraph, and it was originally going to be a collection of them. But when I re-read the pieces, I was so embarrassed at their awfulness and fourteenness that I insisted on re-writing them all, cribbing a few sentences from the original articles here and there. Hence I lumbered myself with a book to write.

When I was twelvish I used to fantasise about writing a

book – I planned out what I would have on the cover, who I would dedicate it to, what I would call it, what I would wear on Wogan etc., it was just the writing of the thing that I thought would be hard.

As it turns out, it's quite the reverse. Titles and covers and bits and pieces are the hassle. Take 'Love-Sixteen' for example. I was in a bit of a quandary because the publishers wanted to call it an A-Z of Problems, or 101 Teenage Problems or something like that. All post-teenagers are obsessed with teenagers having problems. Maybe it's a consolatory measure. Maybe they confuse problems with depression (an adolescent symptom). Thing is, I think I'm pretty much past adolescence now, into my twilight years. So I had to think of another title, and the problems (as a compromise) wound their way into the subtitle. And the subtitle of each chapter. All this misery pressed upon me.

I think the thought behind 'Love-Sixteen' was that I would finish the book while still fifteen. Thus Love-Fifteen, hilarious tennis-based pun, instant best-seller. Not only that, but I would be set up for life (2002: Love-Thirty, 2012: Love-Forty, 2037 – autobiography: My Advantage, or possibly My Game). Sadly, as is often the case, Time's Winged Delivery Van came round with the sixteenth-birthday cake. No pun, no life-structure, everything in ruins. It's now a table tennis-based pun. Not quite as uproarious, I think you'll agree.

Then there was the cover. The first attempt had a picture of some zit cream and a Bros badge on it. The elderly have extremely warped views of youth, I feel. As a minority group, we young are subjected to some nasty prejudices that I would like to see dispelled. As I write I haven't yet seen the final version, but I hear a nasty rumour that there is a picture of me on the front – a backgarden snapshot taken by my friend from round the corner with a Box Brownie, a picture I gave *Them* for purely catalogical purposes. I am wearing, if I remember rightly, a green hat and a pair of cut-off jeans. Everyone will think I dressed (or was dressed) in this self-consciously youthful outfit in order to have my photo taken. Aaarrggghhh, the shame of it. Perhaps they have doctored the picture and put me in evening dress and a tiara. We live in hope.

Then, most traumatic of all decisions, there was the dedication, and all the implications of the choice. 'Why not dedicate it to your mother?' my father keeps saying. (Loose translation: Why not dedicate it to me?) Then there's my brother. But he spotted his name once as I was writing and instructed me not to mention him under any circumstances, and if it was totally unavoidable then he must be referred to solely under the name of Eric. Besides, he won't get around to reading it, so that would be a waste of a good dedication.

I thought of dedicating it to J. D. Salinger (as hero). He dedicated one of his to me, you know. That is to say, he dedicated it to his reader ('If there is an amateur reader still left in the world'). Well, what do you call someone who always skips the Introductions? I'm nothing if not amateur. But he's a recluse and very unlikely to see it. There was Rob Lowe – in the hope that he might pop round to thank me for it in person – and my grandmother was another hot contender. Friends held claims, but the hierarchy is too complicated.

Some books have brilliant long poetic dedications about being taken down from a dusty shelf and so on – but these tend to be aimed at a little god-daughter, and I haven't got one.

The final choice was based on the premise that (even if I do manage to write another book some day) this is my last chance for this particular dedication.

But, because I probably won't manage to w. another b. some day, this is also for Anne and Alan and Eric and J.

Introduction

D. and Rob and Grandma and any little future god-daughter who takes it down from a dusty shelf and, as likely as not, wonders why it's called 'Love-Sixteen', laughs at the hat on the cover, and puts it back again.

1 | Male Order

The Problem of Finding Mr Right

I think I have always been interested in boys. Even the holidays spent in precocious dreams (when I was six or seven) about the son of our cohabiting family were preceded by rather excessive feelings of happiness when my brother was allowed to invite thirty of his little friends round for a party in the back garden and a cake in the shape of a football pitch. I must have been three or four, and yet I was annoyed when my little friend Danielle from around the corner was invited so that I wouldn't be the only girl.

Primary school (aged five to eleven) whizzed by amid glorious mythical tales of holiday romances and boyfriends living in inconvenient places. Then came secondary school and thirteenhood, in which you were actually meant to *do* something with these blokes. There were lots of parties at which you were supposed to get off with as many small boys as possible. The girls who played party games could get through more than twenty in a single night. Happy childhood days. Alice in Wonderland had nothing on this.

I had better explain the expression 'getting off with people', for those who use one of the myriad of other terms. It involves mouths, hands and a dark corner, usually with James Brown playing on the stereo. The mind is (unless you

very, VERY drunk or have got off with this person
any times before) preoccupied with something quite different. For the first five minutes you might be indulging in
a little triumph, or regret, depending on your partner. Then,
as his hands begin to move, you might start worrying that
he is going to unbutton your shirt and you're wearing a
particularly nasty off-white Marks and Spencers bra. You
wonder how you're going to keep the shirt buttoned without appearing unenthusiastic. After this, you might realise
that you're not very comfortable – perhaps the skirting is
digging into your back, or your neck's at an awkward
angle. You want to move in such a way as to neither put
him off completely nor to give him the impression that you
are bored with all this preliminary scrabbling and would
like to be ravaged immediately.

After this, the situation tends to strike me as funny. This
is fatal. Suddenly the whole idea of putting up with this
discomfort is hilarious, I find I am ticklish everywhere. The
worst thing to do at this point is open your eyes, since he
will no doubt have his eyes shut and a very serious set to
his face, which is funnier than anything else. Boys always,
especially sixteen-year-olds, take it so very seriously and I
find myself absolutely engulfed by suppressed mirth. I must
be a very unrewarding inamorata.

Then you both get up, wipe your mouths, give your
crumpled clothes a little tug, exchange phone numbers, take
fond leave of each other and hope you don't bump into
each other again later in the evening in case it spoils the
mood.

Lest I appear unromantic, may I say that it can sometimes
be extremely enjoyable, and it's worth taking the risk.
Sometimes it is like running the last lap of the 1500 metres
– relaxed, and with a satisfying sense of achievement.
(That's how, Steve Cram makes it look anyhow.) Of course,
there will be times when it's more like my experience of

three lengths of swimming the butterfly – uncomfortable and wet.

Speaking of uncomfortable and wet, I suppose I should go further and mention sex. I don't want to say too much, since I intend mine to be a good clean book that you can give your grandmother for Christmas, just to make a change from gloves. Besides, it's a very unimportant thing considering all the fuss people make about it. A few minutes of furtive scrambling, and parents go to such inordinate lengths to stop it, whole books are written about it, whole lunch breaks are spent talking about it. Who has and who hasn't is still a favourite topic for salacious gossip, but there's no challenge in it any more since the answer to the latter is Practically No one. Do you think *she* is sleeping with *him*, people whisper among themselves, pretending that there is the slightest chance of the answer being no. These debaucherous days, teenage virgins are thin on the ground.

Anyway, once the aforementioned petting of varying degrees of heaviness is out of the way, they sometimes come back for more, and then you are meant to go out with them. This is a far harder thing to get right, and much more likely to be like cross-country running – too long, dangerous when it gets dark and every so often a real uphill struggle. I have observed that more people go out with each other than should, but I am sympathetic as I understand the pressures that American films, romantic novels and well-dated friends can put on a girl. Sometimes you just want to be Going Out With Someone, no matter who.

The way I see it, it's bloody hard to find friends of your own sex who are interesting, amusing and similar enough to spend lots of time with – why should it be any easier with the opposite sex? Most people have different rules for friends and boyfriends, the latter being far less exacting. I don't. I rarely go out with anyone.

You're lucky if you come across two funny sixteen-year-old boys in your lifetime. Have you noticed how hard it is to be amusing and eager at the same time? And if there are two things that it's monumentally unattractive to be, it's eager and grateful. Few sixteen-year-old boys are neither. Few of them have a sense of humour, and having a sense of humour is NOT the same as being funny. You can be very witty and entertaining but totally incapable of seeing the funny side of dropped crockery, being too late to catch a train, miscalculated comments etc. If you don't believe me, ask my father.

It's nice if someone is intelligent too – which doesn't mean pretending he's making spur-of-the-moment acute observations which it's perfectly obvious he's quoting from the history essay he wrote the week before! Or worse, the history essay which Jeremy, the school swot, lent him to crib from.

I also have to admit that I am predisposed to gentlemanliness. I'm a pushover for it. Those overly-eager boys who make those untempting offers as they ferret about in your clothing – little do they realise that if they held the bedroom door open for me I might be more tempted. In principle it's a little daft, and I laugh when my brother is chastised for not standing up when a woman enters the room, but somehow when someone holds an umbrella for me or walks on the outside in the street then, to quote Marilyn Monroe, 'My spine turns to custard, I get goosepimply all over, and I come to 'em.' Sadly, you don't come across that much. The only really gentlemanly bloke I know lives in South Africa. There's a limit to where a girl can go to be helped off with her coat.

Then there's how he feels about you. I can never make up my mind whether it's more attractive when someone is in love with you or totally indifferent. When I was twelveish

I definitely thought the latter, now it seems like so much hassle. Unrequited love gets boring after a while.

But you need to decide which of the two is more attractive so that you can be it yourself when attempting a seduction. And you want your friends to be well-prepared. If he is going to ask you out, you see, you want to have told them that you think he's amazing so that they fully appreciate the meaning of his request. You don't, however, want to keep telling them you're in love with people who end up going out with someone else – one of the clued-up friends if you're not careful.

So, what have I said I'm looking for? Intelligent, funny, (WITH a sense of humour), well-mannered if at all possible. How do you recognise these traits under flashing lights and over thumping music? I don't know, which is why I'm wary of picking up blokes in nightclubs. All you have to go on is their personal appearance, so how can you help a little bias towards the more physically attractive? You can't. Not only are you risking your own self-respect by expecting someone to pick you out on physical merits, but you are running a serious risk of ending up with a quite good-looking dork. Your phone will ring a couple of evenings later and there he'll be, a voice like Mickey Mouse and no face (that you can remember) to redeem him. Even so, you might arrange to meet him for a drink, just in case, in which case you will be letting yourself in for an evening of monolithic embarrassment and boredom. There will be one or two oases of conversation, thick with relief, followed by vast empty deserts. It's a dangerous business.

In a way, though, going out with someone you already know well can be even worse. Suddenly you might find that there is nothing at all to say, while there was plenty before, and the moment of physical contact (which should feel like a final expression of long-pent-up passion) is far more likely to feel strange and not particularly pleasant.

Holiday romances have far better chances of success. Since you know you will never see him again when the two weeks are over, you can be much more relaxed and carefree. Neither of you is likely to be behaving like you normally do at home, so you will both be having a fling with someone who doesn't actually exist. Which is very comforting when you go home thinking that no bloke of your acquaintance could ever live up to it, why does Mr Right have to live 9000 miles away etc. etc. You forget him in a month, perhaps you will exchange a few half hearted letters about what's happening at school (written by both of you with the help of the French/German/Italian dictionary, so they are unlikely to be fluent and interesting, e.g. 'When I returned to my dwelling I was very crestfallen, I feel the loss of you') but that'll be it. I have heard horror stories of holiday romances turning up unheralded on doorsteps, but that (mercifully) does not happen often. He usually has more sense.

Meanwhile you struggle on with British boys, every week lowering your standards a little more and accepting a little less. Ah well, some day the right one will come along – intelligent, funny, courteous, you name it – and you'll get married and live happily ever after. Yeah, and one day *London Plus* will be interesting.

2 Anything Illegal Considered

The Age Limit Problem

One of the things that we Young Ones like to gripe about is the age limit of certain activities. Let's face it, when you're still at school, living at home, funded entirely by pocket money, there aren't many great wrongs done you by the State. We can't complain about taxes and wages, motorways and house prices and rates. Not much is asked of us in the general legislature. We are not forced to *do* anything particularly unpleasant, so what can we complain about? What we're forced *not* to do.

Of course, the things we are by law not supposed to do are, by and large, the things that social pressures very much expect us to do.

Now take the cinema. Does anyone really think that no fourteen-year-old ever goes to a '15' film? Preposterous.

I saw my first '15' film when I was about twelve. It was *Another Country* at the Kensington Odeon. I slathered on the make-up and borrowed a pair of thick glasses. They were my mother's idea – she insisted that I looked several years older with them on. In the foyer, my parents bought the tickets while I slouched about by the stairs, looking like something from a PG Tips' advert. Being, at twelve, a

peculiarly honest person, I felt very guilty about this decep-
tion, and I thought it an apt penance to keep the glasses
on throughout the film. I swayed out with my eyesight
seriously impaired and no idea whether I'd seen *Ben Hur*
or *Bambi*.

I saw my first '18' film when I was fourteen. That was
some sort of supernatural chainsaw film – you know the
one, where the half-man half-beast lurks by the summer
camp with a pocketful of eyeballs and a thirst for cheerlead-
ers' blood. I remain relatively uncorrupted. My desire to
maim and kill is more keenly aroused by Little and Large.

There is a sort of complacency among adults concerning
on-screen sex and violence: 'Well, it's okay as long as the
kids don't see it.' What a ludicrous attitude. Surely the sort
of person who would be turned on by cinematic violence,
sexual or otherwise, enough to re-create it, is that type of
person whatever their age? And isn't the biggest threat to
a non-violent community, men over eighteen years of age?
Not fourteen-year-old girls anyway.

Which would suggest that banning children from 'dangerous' films does not decrease violence. Either a film is per-
ilous to the mentally weak or it is not. If it is, then it
should be banned universally, not just kept from kids. When
someone hits eighteen, they do not automatically become
immune to outside influences. Have you ever noticed, by
the way, that it's only old people who are actually offended
by sex, violence and bad language? We kids love a bit of
gratuity.

Besides, when I was fourteen (if I can cast my mind back
over, what, two years now? Two years-and-a-half? How
time flies!) I looked exactly fourteen, no older no younger,
yet I had no trouble at all getting into '18' films, buying
alcohol, entering nightclubs (I led a wild life at fourteen!).
Try and pay child-rate fare on the bus without my under-
sixteen Travelcard, however, and I would be thrown face

down onto Finchley Road and told I was lucky to get off
without a court summons.

Furthermore, banning us little tykes with brains like mod-
elling clay from the more obvious media certainly doesn't
keep us fresh and innocent. Our parents, and our nanny
society, may dictate which films we should see, which parts
of the body we should be aware of, which words we should
hear, which books we may handle without great passages
Tipp-exed out, but have you noticed that nothing is ever
said about *radio*?

Something about its relative old age must lead parents to
believe that it is, if not entirely educational, almost universally beneficial. My parents thrill to think of me tucked away
in my room with the radio on, listening, perhaps, to *The
Henry Hall Show* or *Gladys Hay* or possibly *Troyes and
his Mandoliers*.

No, when I wish them sweet dreams on a Monday evening and hurtle upstairs, cup of tea in hand, I am not
heading eagerly for *Monday Night at Eight*, but that pin-
nacle of moral guidance, the lightbulb of information in
the unlit hall of my carnal knowledge, the very summit
of induction into adulthood, Philip Hodson's *Sexual and
Marital Problems* programme on LBC.

These are not, of course, Philip Hodson's *own* sexual and
marital problems (does God have an inferiority complex?)
but the S&M problems (an unfortunate, though not
inappropriate, abbreviation) of the public, which the magical Mr Hodson solves in exactly fifteen minutes, between
commercial breaks.

It is impossible to convey through the printed word the
vast range of sexual deviants who pass, metaphorically
speaking, through Mr Hodson's capable hands. He has an
antidote for every available kind of quirk and kink, every
fetish and foible, every vagary and whim. He has discussed
parts of the body that you're embarrassed to let *yourself*

see. He has described techniques that make the *Kama Sutra* look like *Mansfield Park*. Believe me, three years' worth of Monday nights have educated me in areas which a Triple-X Swedish au pair movie could hardly touch on. I have learnt an awful lot more from Ted in Blackheath and Prudence in Golders Green than I ever could from *A Hot Night in Bangkok*.

I phoned Phil once. It was a rainy night in 1984, the parents were out, I was lying in bed puzzling out the best way to let Harry, a charming sixteen-year-old whom I had befriended on my bus route, down gently on the romantic front, when it occurred to me that the answer might lie in a simple conversation with Uncle Hodson. I dialled. I hung up. I re-dialled. It rang. I hung up. I re-dialled. It rang. Someone answered. I hung up. I re-dialled. It rang. Someone answered. Someone asked me to outline my problem. I started with my age. Someone said 'You're *TWELVE*??!!**!?!' I hung up. I never rang again.

But the silliest age rules of all must be the pub laws. When you're fourteen – and this is the technical bit so you can skip it if you like – you can enter a pub but you cannot buy a drink. Not even a milkshake. Not even a prawn cocktail Skip. You can *drink* a drink, if you find one lying about, or if someone buys one for you, but you cannot physically pay for one. When you're sixteen you can buy a soft drink, and when you're eighteen you may buy anything you like.

In other words, the Great Lawmakers have decided that it is safer for a fourteen-year-old to stand outside the pub and persuade a strange bloke to buy her a drink, than it is for her to buy it herself. Eminently sensibler, I'm sure you'll agree.

Another option for your streetwise kid is to buy a soft drink from the grocer's next door to the pub and drink it in the car park. A peculiarly untempting idea for spending an evening I find. Perhaps it's just me.

It's all rather odd considering the attempts made to woo young people into pubs. Cocktaily drinks, modern music, fruit machines . . . the pub is no longer for the middle-aged.

Now I'm sixteen, of course, a wealth of exciting illogicality opens up in my path. I may now get married, yet not take my husband for a drive. I can have sex, yet I cannot watch it on screen. I can start a family but I cannot vote. I can leave school and take a full-time job to support myself, but I cannot leave home without my parents' consent. I have to admit I am slightly confused as to my role in society, adulthoodwise.

Oh, by the way, I had to deal with the Harry problem Hodsonless in the end. After a few weeks he asked me straight out if I 'had a crush on him', I said no, he looked rather embarrassed and we never saw each other again, to speak to. Who knows, if I had got through to Philip we might have been setting up home together at this moment.

Blast.

3 | Scene and Herd

The Fashion Problem

I am not a slave to fashion. I do not read fashion magazines. You would not catch me shaving my head and wearing wedgies because Vivien Westwood suggested that I do so.

That is not to say that I am not self-conscious. A year or so ago I might have won an award for total continuous embarrassment. Now at the wizened age of sixteen, of course, adolescence is loosening its grip somewhat and I am not SO embarrassed SO much of the time, but I am still occasionally to be found banging my head on the bathroom wall and vowing never to go out in public again.

Falling over does it every time. That's the worst. When I was sixish, I couldn't run four metres in a straight line without falling over and rushing to the school secretary and her bottle of witch hazel. With my Prussian Blue ribbed tights held away from a battle-scarred knee, I didn't mind falling over at all. I sported my green scabs like medals. Now that I do it rather less often, a single trip can ruin the next week of my life.

Friends don't help either. Kate and Jessica love to remind me of a time when they insisted we ran for a bus that was stuffed with fellow Paulines and Paulinas (that means girls from my school and boys from the school over the bridge.

Don't worry, we don't have many terms like that, we're not one of those schools where they rush about saying, '*Cave*, we must get to Green for station or Old Cheese will be pissed off,' but we had to have some kind of shorthand for Girls From The Girls' School and Boys From The Boys' School). Anyway, I fell over really quite dramatically – not a dainty trip but the full flat-on-the-floor, history books strewn across Hammersmith Broadway, traffic stops, a crowd gathers sort-of-fall. Bad enough, you might think, but Kate and Jess have reminded me of it at regular intervals ever since. What are friends for? God knows.

I had to have my photograph taken once, to go with a piece I had written for a magazine. I was a very poised model, I must say, standing on Hampstead Heath, oblivious to the curious passers-by. (And on Hampstead Heath, you get some VERY curious passers-by). Everything was perfect until I had to get out of the car back at home. I said an elegant goodbye, stepped out, dropped my gloves in a puddle, laughed it off charmingly and slammed the door on my coat. So I then had to open the door and say goodbye again. I hate saying goodbye twice.

Every day Jessica and I say goodbye to each other, then she crosses the road, and we continue for about five minutes on opposite sides of the road, pretending we've forgotten about each other so as to avoid leave-taking again. It's ludicrous. Will I grow out of this behaviour? Or do adults do it too?

Luckily, as I get older I *am* becoming slightly more grace-ful. Rudolf Nureyev has little to worry about, but I'm getting there.

It's not that I'm getting less selfconscious but as I say, I don't follow fashion. I'm not a *deviant* (although I know these tendencies are rife in adolescents) but I'm not a victim either.

I did not – and I bet there are few who can say this –

buy a Filofax at any point in 1987. I withstood the pressure, I stuck with my Little Pocket Diary (you know the sort: hardly any room for dates and phone numbers, but pages and pages of information at beginning and end. Maps of Gibraltar, conversion tables, what the time is in China, how to tie a reef knot. That sort of diary). I ought to admit though, that part of the reason why I never bought a Filo (I can still use the jargon) was that I missed all the hints on the *Daily Mail* Women's Page until it was too late, and we were into Fashion Bracket Two.

There's Bracket One, when all the very fashionable people get hold of the new item, on the sly; then there's Bracket Two when all the trying-hard-to-be-fashionable people get it. Bracket Three when it's too late, everyone's got it, and hot on the heels of Three comes Bracket Four when it's the most untrendy thing in the world to have, and everyone who's anyone has thrown theirs away. I missed Filofax Bracket One, and of course they're now almost Fiveish – you feel old if you even know what it is.

Filofaxes at school annoyed me intensely anyway. People sat with their fat Filos open in front of them, hoping desperately that their neighbours would admire the inordinate number of male names in the addresses bit or the almost incredible number of social engagements in the diary bit. Some people kept pictures of themselves tucked into the front of their Filofax, with one corner peeking enticingly out, showing them squashed into a photo-booth with four friends ('That was just *such* a laugh, I swear Sophie was sitting *right* on my left leg, I nearly died, I'm not joking'). All intensely irritating.

By 'fashion' of course, people often mean clothing. I find words like 'trendy', 'fashionable', 'in' etc, irritating. (Let's face it, I find life irritating).

My mother asks me every so often if various things that I say/wear/do are 'in', and I can't think of a greater insult.

And buying clothes with parents is agony – if you don't like the length of a skirt they say, 'Well, that's how they're wearing them at the moment' – as if I really cared how anyone else was wearing anything.

Make-up's the same way. Every so often you get magazine spreads telling you that, 'bright colours are the thing this season', or, 'put away those purples, pastel pinks are prevailing!' Who really wears 'fashionable' make-up?

Not that I am necessarily an authority. Personally, I am quite happy with the way I wear make-up – but it is not unknown for my brother to take a look at my completed face and ask me if I've been in a fight, and he has once or twice remarked that my lipstick puts him in mind of the old days of *Crackerjack* when the kids had to remove a key from a vat of jam with their teeth. Still, what do you expect from a brother?

Then there's dieting. Thin is in. Fat hasn't, of course, been in since the Restoration – life must've been wonderful then. Biting straight into a roast boar and knowing it's only assisting your beauty routine.

I have to admit I am a victim of puppy fat. Now, I don't want to dwell on this – I dwell in it as it is – but I do labour under the curse of 'girlish plumpness', you know, the sort that older people think is lovely, just what they found attractive when they were a lad.

I'm very good at planning diets. I draw wonderful timetables and eating/exercising plans, sketch little borders around them, then put them at the back of a drawer and forget about it. I have tried set diets, but they're no good, especially the ones where you get to eat two bits of cardboard once a day or, worse, 'the nourishing drink – strawberry or chocolate flavoured' which are pure hell. I sent off for a Michael van Straten LBC diet, but it's impossible to follow if you don't have access to all the right foods. Surprisingly, 'Cream of celery soup, stewed raisins, baked parsnips, China tea with lemon' are not always available in the school canteen. I tried taking my own, but everything got cold and there's something unappealing about eight-hour-old China tea in a Snoopy thermos left over from the cub scouts. There's the old favourite, the Seafood Diet (when you seafood you eat it) which I have been following for some time now, but little is happening. Even when I do lose weight scales-wise, the puppy fat doesn't lessen.

Besides, it's very difficult to handle at school. The school doctor is absolutely paranoid about anorexia. Every time you go in for a medical they point out that you've lost half-a-pound, why, it could be dangerous etc. etc. Last time, the doctor showed me a chart which stated that it would be bad for me to go under nine stone. Nine stone! And I'm a midget.

The family don't help either. Parents and grandparents love to see a bit of good healthy flesh. Brothers are best ('Don't you worry about being harpooned?') but it's not exactly comforting.

Girls' magazines are a joke. All the Agony Aunts and beauty writers are so trendy, they do nothing but insist that a boy who doesn't lust after you when you're fat, greasy and covered in spots is not worth looking twice at anyway.

I hate low-calorie food. It's the way they try and pretend it's normal food, just magically less fattening. Have you ever tried those sugar-free baked beans? Absolutely vile. And diet colas – who'd drink those when they can have water? It's the enticing label on the bottle proclaiming that the whole bottle of cola contains one calorie that does it – you think, just as long as I don't get the glass with the calorie in it, I'm all right.

I don't much like vegetables either. This was a bit of a problem, since I used to be a vegetarian. It was when I was ten, I suddenly had a massive rush of guilt about small furry things being wrenched away from their mothers and served up with chips. I tacked anti-vivisection posters all over the school. I sent protesting letters to the Canadian Prime Minister about seal culling. I insisted to everyone I met that you could live without meat. *You* probably can, but *I* certainly couldn't. I lived on Frosties and spaghetti for a year, then I ran into McDonalds for a fix and my Animal Liberation days were over. I am very ashamed of myself for abandoning my principles like that, but it was getting ridiculous. You know those cartoons where the cat looks at the bird and sees a platter of roast meat? I was living it. I realised one day in Biology, watching my lab partner slicing through a sheep's heart and thinking how delicious it looked, that I could be green no longer.

But enough of food and dieting I'm only getting hungry and depressed and onto other aspects of trend.

There's music. Ho yes, street cred is very dependent on *in* sounds. This, again, depends on who you are and where you are – no doubt there are places where Brother Beyond is a good name to drop. I hope never to visit them. Intellectual snobbery abounds in music – the worst are people who like U2 and The Smiths, and think they're 'fringe' and that Bono should be Prime Minister. I have no objection to people liking them, I am a non-value-judgement person, but it's the ones who think they know about music and are better than everyone else because of their obtuse Smiths and U2 albums that really get to me. If they want to be fringe, why not go for Jason and the Scorchers, Kilburn and the High Roads, Rape Man? (Actually, I've never heard any Rape Man, they were mentioned to me the other night by a bloke I know when I had asked him swishly, 'What he would like to hear?' - I was suitably put in my place.)

But, of course, while many people feel far too superior about their musical tastes, too many are too quick to be embarrassed about them. Stand up for your beliefs! Say out loud 'I bought *Starting Together* by Su Pollard, and I'm proud of it.' So many teenagers, for example, just loved Wham! but kept it to themselves because they were over-popular and boppy. 1985 was rife with latent Wham! fans, and then in 1987, when George Michael's solo album was pronounced 'pretty good' by acceptable people, thus making it possible for all those cool cats to buy it, you could feel the ripple of relief.

It was all right, by the way, to go to the Wham! farewell concert. Different rules apply there. You may have noticed the flocks of people who had never in their lives listened to a Jean Michel Jarré record, if they had heard of him at all, who were suddenly desperate to get their hands on a ticket for his Docklands shows. I couldn't understand it. All I knew was that he was something to do with Charlotte Rampling.

I rarely go to concerts. I've never been to a massive superstar extravaganza-type concert, of the Michael Jackson/Madonna ilk. I went to a Don McLean one once. That was brilliant. It was at the Royal Festival Hall and our tickets were double-booked. The best they could offer, said the ticket-lady apologetically, was the Royal Box. Catherine and I consulted lengthily and decided that, under the circumstances, we could probably muddle through somehow. Our previous seats had not commanded a par-ticularly good view, since they were behind some of Don's bigger fans.

Two of the Royal Box seats were already taken. Hello, I thought, not only in the Royal Box, but with real Royals. Unfortunately they were not real Royals. They were not even real boxers. They were a quiet couple who did not join in the communal singing of 'American Pie' and, since Catherine did not know the words, I soon lapsed into silence myself. Probably not before shattering any illusions the couple might have been nurturing about my own Royal status.

The music of today, generally, is not good. We spend a lot of time at school surfing in waves of nostalgia about the early eighties music. Adam and the Ants. Blondie. Now that's what I call proper popular music.

Although I did go through a VERY BRIEF New Romantic phase at that time. Yes, it's true, I was a Duran Duran fan. I had my black velvet knickerbockers and my red-and-gold bandanna. I liked the music, but they weren't my pin-ups – Shakin' Stevens was. Yes, every inch of wall space was covered with Shakin'. What do you want? I was eight.

I think it was a Gary Numan song that ran, 'New Romantics are oh so boring' that jolted me out of that phase. I quite liked Gary, but there's always been a slight guilt attached to his name because my brother Giles and I once pretended to a mother's help that we had met him on holiday. We even wrote her a letter 'from him' which she pinned above her bed. God, I hate myself. I don't think we ever confessed – she is, possibly, even now casting her book aside and ripping Gary's letter off the wall. We were wicked children.

Nowadays, to return to the subject, everything is synthesised Stock Aitken Waterman and sung by soap stars, not real music like when I were a lass. The youth of today, tut tut, what are they coming to? My children certainly won't be listening to any of this rap rubbish, not if they want to live under my roof they won't. Any one of my kids who dares walk through my door in cycling shorts, a cap on backwards and a belt with its name on is going right back out into the street.

Still, by the time I have children it'll all have changed again anyway, so why worry? Today's trend is tomorrow's Fashion Bracket Two. It even happens in the Bible – 'The fashion of this world passeth away' (Corinthians). You can take it as gospel.

4 Small Change

Problems and Exchanges

The word 'Exchange' strikes terror into many an adolescent heart.

I don't think I have ever come across anyone who has made contact with someone purely for the purposes of Exchanging, and really got on with them. The usual scenario: English girl goes to France, spends ten days copiously avoiding all French-speakers, returns even worse than before, spends next few months dreading imminent arrival of French girl with similar designs.

Its always painful when the Other Half comes to England. I remember when Soraya's hated twosome (double the agony, she was really after some self-torture) came across from France to improve their English. We were all biased against them from the start, having received tormented postcards from Soraya's visit there, with grotesque carica- tures of the family and desperate cries for help. We did *try* to be welcoming – but it was an uphill struggle. One evening in particular springs to mind, an evening when we all went to a party in Park Lane at about eleven p.m. The music was terrible but catchy and, after about four hours dancing, we wondered where the French girls had got to. We found them sitting on the doorstep of the house, chatting in very uncomplimentary-sounding French. We went to mad lengths to try to lure them into the party – we begged, we threatened, we tried it in French, we tried it in German, we acted out the fun of the dancing, we looked close to tears. Nothing. *Rien. Nicht.*

You get the guilt-trip Exchanges as well – they're the worst. They sit on their beds all day ('Don't worry about me, I'll just sit here and browse through my English dictionary') and perform the same rigmarole every time they want to go anywhere.

Exchange: I want to go to the Madame Tussauds.'
English: We went there yesterday, don't you remember?
Exchange: I want to go again. I like it.
English: You *don't* like it. You cried when we had to queue for two hours, you made a scene because Mitterand had a mole in the wrong place, you thought all the models were 'si *mal formé*' and we had to leave after twelve minutes.
Exchange: I change my mind.
English (resignedly):   All right then, let's go.
Exchange: No, no, no, no, not if you don't want.
English: If you want to go again, we'll go again.
Exchange: I don't want to be trouble. We watch *Neighbours* now as you suggest.
English: Françoise, it's *your* holiday, we'll do what *you* want.
Exchange: Don't worry about me, I'll just sit here and browse through my English dictionary . . .

The daftest Exchange I ever witnessed was that of my brother Giles and a boy from Munich, whom we shall call Hans. (A rather optimistic handle, if I remember him rightly).

The German party came to England for a month, two weeks into which the English group left for Germany. That meant that the burden of entertaining the Exchanges fell upon the poor siblings left behind. At that time, a year before I started learning German, I couldn't speak a word of it. *Now*, of course, I have been learning German for two years. And I still can't speak a word of it.

I looked forward to his arrival with great excitement – a sixteen-year-old man living in our house for a month! I washed my hair and slapped on what I thought, at thirteen, was a very skilful and attractive make-up. (Peacock blue eyeshadow and fuschia lip gloss).

Of course, he turned out to be small, with a pudding-bowl haircut and thick glasses. No matter, the liberal mind which was, at thirteen, already in the bud, was well prepared to fall madly in love with his amazing personality.

Disappointed.

He differed totally from most of the English boys I know (including my brother) on the cleanliness front. Giles wears the same torn jeans and T-shirt every day, with hair long and unbrushed, to suggest tramphood, but is in fact almost obsessively clean. (Ask me how many times the shower has gone freezing cold as I stand beneath it, hair thick with Vosene, because he has been in it for the past seven hours). Hans, however, dressed very smartly and combed his hair with scientific precision, but he didn't open that bathroom door or touch that tap during the entire four weeks' stay.

Besides which, he had clearly been brought up to believe that, as a male, he had no role in household choring whatsoever. My mother put his meals before him and watched as he gobbled them wordlessly down and disappeared to watch *Black Forest Clinic*. If my parents were out, *I* had the honour of cooking, serving and washing up. I am not sure whether it was because the liberal mind which prepared to embrace his personality had not yet grasped the unfettering of women, or whether it was just that I was flattered to be counted as a woman, but I made no murmur of complaint. Just served. As is my métier.

Giles had a great time, romancing Hans's surprisingly large circle of female friends, knocking off school at two in the afternoon and being smothered with luxury by Mrs Hans. The poor chap must have been shattered to come home to this feminist fortress where he is expected to lay the table, make grateful noises over food and at least *offer* to help with the washing-up. No doubt Hans staggered over his threshold when the month was up, half-dead with the need of some good nourishing knackwurst, served up by a hausfrau with a golden spoon. His mother probably thought we maltreated him terribly.

Now, *I* went about it the right way.

I met my Exchange, Florence, on holiday in Spain. We got to know each other, we liked each other, we traded a few letters, *then* we planned some mutual visiting.

She came to us first. I think her main worry was that we would live in a small house. She told me that her father had reassured her: if we could afford that hotel, we must be all right.

Perhaps it lost something in the translation.

I felt like an ambassador while she was here. I had a strong sense that I must show her the best that England has to offer and send her back glowing with enthusiasm and envy.

It rained.

We waited hours for buses.

She came to school on a day when we had double physics.

She noticed that the salad in the canteen was more densely populated than Glasgow.

I was ill.

Someone told a joke about the Heysel stadium, thinking Flo was French. She's from Belgium, her house is only kilometres from Heysel.

BUT we had a great time. It was brilliant. Everyone was jealous of my luck, and liked her immensely. She had been to London before so we didn't have to tramp round looking at the crown jewels and Piccadilly circus – we just went to see films and pottered about like any normal pair of friends, which was the best way for her to learn English after all.

Although one thing *was* embarrassing – my total inability to find my way round London. She knew it better than I did. Several times I was forced to look aghast at the sky and shriek, 'Goodness me, what on earth is that?' so that I could consult my map as she stared up, muttering, '*Je ne voie rien.*'

After which, it was *my* turn to go to Belgium.

I had never been on a plane by myself before, I felt very professional. Very much the *Daily Mail* Ideal Woman. I hoped I might meet, by some freak of fate, an amazingly goodlooking sixteen/seventeen-year-old man also on his way to Belgium but usually based somewhere in the Cricklewood area. Bad luck. The closest I came was my left-hand neighbour, a large Dutchman who looked like a cheese. In the nicest possible way. Then I was in the don't-want-to-be-rude-but-would-prefer-just-to-sit-silently-reading-my-Jackie-Collins-and-eating-my-boiled-sweets situation, as he chatted about what he had been up to in London.

Just before we were due to land, I was suddenly struck with a terrible fear that I would not recognise Florence. I had spent a large proportion of a two-week holiday in her company, she had stayed with me in London, I was in possession of several photographs of her – yet I had totally forgotten what she looked like. I was tempted to stay on the plane and wait for the trip back, but I don't think they work like buses.

Hoping fervently that she had a vague idea of what *I* looked like, I wandered out into a mass of Belgians.

Of course, I recognised her immediately – although I didn't recognise the language she was speaking. Turned out to be French. I wondered if I could speak French. I wasn't quite certain, but I didn't think I could. Luckily, after the Gallic greeting, Florence and her father switched to an English which was better than mine and, feeling that I ought to be trying to speak French but appreciating that it was a physical impossibility, I relaxed.

I was suddenly tired after the flight and the last thing I felt like doing was sightseeing, so when we pulled up outside some sort of Belgian equivalent to the Tower of London, my heart sank. Then I realised this was their house. I wished I had worn an evening dress and silk stockings.

Florence's mother appeared at the moat.

She ushered me in to the drawing room where a large tea was laid out. Now, while Florence had been staying with me, she had shown an immense fondness for Mr Kipling's Manor House Cake. Before my departure from London I had nipped into Waitrose and bought one to take along with me as a little joke.

Since this tea was waiting there, I thought it might be a good time to introduce the cake so I fumbled with the straps of my suitcase. It sprang open and an article of clothing fell out. I can't remember quite what it was, but some radiant example of English chic. A vest, I think.

Anyway, I rummaged about in the carpet and stuffed the item back into my suitcase. Mrs Florence (Florence and Mr Florence had disappeared) was peering down from her chair with a puzzled expression.

I extracted the now rather battered box containing the cake and put it on the table. The joke seemed suddenly less funny.

'It is what?' enquired Maman, politely.

'Um, um,' (it had been a long time since I had aired my French), '*C'est un gâteau, par* Mr Kipling. *Florence l'aimait quand elle était en Angleterre.*'

Maman smiled generously. She removed the crumbling cake from the box, put it on a plate which was rather too large for it, and placed it in the middle of the table, among the precision-cut sandwiches, millefeuilles and expensive glossy pastries. God, I empathised with it. I wanted to take it outside to compare notes.

Luckily, Florence then reappeared and shrieked with delight when she saw the Manor House cake, and the parents kindly helped themselves to a large slice each. If they exchanged amused glances, I didn't see them.

Conversation was rather stilted over tea, and there was plenty of silent chewing and looking away into the distance. The talk came out in little dollops, whenever we did hit a conversational patch the air was thick with relief and over-enthusiasm.

I then retired to the guest suite to unpack.

One thing for which Belgium is appalling, I have to admit, is the Teenage Diet. There is chocolate *everywhere*. In the estate agents. Pushed on street corners. Thrust at you from alleyways. And not your common-or-garden fruit and nut bars that you get here, either – even the slot machines produce the luxurious fresh-cream kind. My get-slim-for-the-holiday plan took the first tram back to London, abandoning me in a chocolate haven beyond the dreams of even Roald Dahl.

As we chewed, we also tramped. I had not been to Belgium before so Florence was under obligation to show me all the typical Belgian sights. There is a statue called the Mannequin Pis which seems to form the core of Belgian sightseeing. It stands just off the main square in Brussels and depicts a small boy taking a leak into a fountain. Not quite Nelson's Column. There is a museum in the square itself which houses hundreds of copies of this small boy, dressed in various national costumes, but in the same dignified pose. I admired it profusely. I know which side my bread's buttered.

It may just be that the Florences are very much higher-

caste than we are, but it seems that there is a much wider
gulf between the classes in Belgium than there is here. Florence mixes only with those teenagers whose names figure
on a list which is held by all the rich Mamans in Brussels.
Each listed family takes it in turn to entertain this group of
princes and princesses by holding a ball or a party. Florence
is expected to marry one of them with all speed. I am told
that the same applies to debs in this country, but the Belgians start much earlier.

One day, on a tram, Flo and I were watchless, and I
suggested asking a man in the seat across the aisle what the
time was. Flo gave me shocked look, and put her finger to
her lips. When we alighted she explained that this man was
'not appropriate'. I am not sure whether she worried more
that he was a potential kidnapper, or that he would take
any communication as a signal of friendship. I asked her
how she could tell (he looked perfectly respectable to me)
but she just shook her head, 'You can tell'.

I did have one argument with her on that front. We were
braving the bumper cars at Walibi amusement park, taking
it in turns to drive. When Florence was at the wheel, we
steered elegantly around the outside, brushing nothing, as
if it were a leisurely drive through the countryside. When
it was my turn I hurtled us into the middle, trained by
sixteen years of Hampstead Fair, bouncing and bruising us
umpteen times a minute. There was one particular car,
driven by two boys, which careered into us several times.
Florence snatched the wheel firmly and guided us out of
the mêlée. As before, we alighted and I stood humbly waiting for my lecture. It appeared that my behaviour was quite
inappropriate for ladies of our standing – people would
assume that we were rather fast and not at all well-bred.
Why, I wondered, did we choose to try the bumper cars at
all? No acceptable reply forthcoming, Florence and I did
have a little spat. It ended quickly since I knew it was not

really her fault and there was no point trying to convert her (I have enough of preaching to the unconvertible when I am at school) and she thought it undecorous to have a row in a public place.

For the rest of the week we tried not to refer to that incident, and got on brilliantly. I think my French improved, but Florence's English is so good that she had trouble in stopping herself lapsing into it on a regular basis. It was true of the whole family. I would not have been surprised to learn that they spoke English even while alone, for the sake of practice. It appeared to be a great struggle for them all, even the eight-year-old brother, to stick to French. This problem extended to the lifestyle as well – they made a tremendous effort to re-create England for me in as many areas as possible. They firmly believed that the English like their meat, 'very well dern', and I had a lump in my throat as I watched the cook (!), every evening, cutting a couple of slices off the beef and charring them specially for me.

Florence's mother had bought what she thought was special English tea – it was a carton of strange teabags that gave off an odd earthy flavour. None of the rest of the family would touch this exceptional, expensive tea and I found myself in the position of drinking large mugs of it on the hour so as not to offend anyone. It was so lovely of them to try and put their ideas of England into practice that I didn't want to suggest either that their notions were wrong or that I was actually there to experience Belgium.

The most surprising point of the week was a very reassuring one. They revere the English in an incredible way. The media insist that everyone in Europe thinks of the English as Union Jack T-shirt-wearing football hoodlums who consume vast quantities of chips and lager in order to throw them up over defenseless old ladies later in the evening.

If this is the case in Europe, generally, it certainly wasn't in Belgium – and let's not forget that my visit was only a year or so after Heysel (a disaster which, *Fawlty Towers*-like, I took great pains to avoid discussing).

The only general beliefs that my hosts held about the English were old-fashioned pleasing ones: that we all wear Burberry overcoats, that we eat muffins and read Sherlock Holmes, that we carry clean pocket handkerchiefs and play golf and stand up for the national anthem, that we watch lots of cricket and are terribly polite.

It was very odd hearing all this since, although I had gone to Belgium in the same ambassadorial spirit with which I had welcomed Florence to England, determined to shatter the awful prejudices I was sure they would have, I found the roles totally reversed – and it was me who finished that exchange with a renewed faith in my compatriots and a re-established delight in Being English.

5 | Sects and the Single Girl

Problems with Cliques and Connections

I have always told my parents the truth about my social life. I have never seen much reason not to.

But, for many of my friends, it seems innate to employ a little amount of euphemism when describing an evening's entertainment to their parents. Of course, I have *tried* keeping things from THEM from time to time, but it rarely works out. I remember a time when we were all going to the Camden Palace (an over-eighteens club in, yes, Camden which is best on a Wednesday night, which will explain why your daughter's school concerts, friends' birthdays etc. all fall on a Wednesday) and everyone seemed to be telling their parents that they were going to a friend's dinner party. In fact, I organised with one friend that I would phone her house at 6:03 pm, when she would make sure she was in the bath, and say to her mother, 'I just wanted to check that ******* was coming to *****'s dinner party tonight.' Naturally enough, I gave mine the same story. The next day, racked with guilt and wondering whether to punish myself by deliberately missing *Neighbours*, I confessed to my mother what I had actually been up to. She was rather puzzled as to my motives for calling it a dinner party in the first place, and had no objection at all to my going to Camden. It was a particularly good *Neighbours* that day.

I have observed, and this is strictly between you and me, that those girls whose parents are very heavy with the rules and curfews, tend to behave worse. Surely most parents realise that what you can do at one in the morning at Camden you can do much more conveniently at three in the afternoon at a friend's house? Although I appreciate that parents are a lot more innocent than we usually give them credit for. Some girls in my year wanted to put on, 'Come back to the five-and-dime, Jimmy Dean' for a school play this year, but apparently it mentions the word(s) 'sex-change' and we were told the parents wouldn't be able to cope. So it looks like *the Importance of Being Earnest* for the thirty-fourth time. Bags not Dr Chasuble. But I'm digressing from my major point, which is, the fact that girls who must be home by ten o'clock every Saturday night get up to a lot less good than those who are allowed home whenever they like. Girls whose parents treat them like adults make much more rewarding daughters. Of course I am generalising wildly – and, let's face it, an element of desperate persuasion is creeping in.

The social cliques at school (you'd be surprised how many cliques there are within the one large clique that we schoolgirls are supposed to be) split up into what people like to do on their Saturday nights.

There is the group that likes to 'mellow out' at someone's house, involving the use of certain substances . . .

This is an amiable, if rather daft, little social clump, and there is something appealing in their gentle ambitions ('We're all going to live in a big house in a field of magic mushrooms'). Some people can't stand this group because it's, '*so* affected', which of course it is, but I reckon it's better than wanting to be an accountant.

The main tragedy of this group's life is the amount of money that most of them command. They dress in paint-splattered old jeans and dusty bits of material to hold back the scrupulously unbrushed hair, and where the buttons have popped off the jackets there are badges proclaiming undying faith in Nelson Mandela and cries to Legalise It. Everyone knows, however, that many of these would-be tramps are in fact raking in the £100 allowance every week and trotting faithfully down to the Bradford and Bingley to put it in the Nice Little VolksWagen fund.

Similarly, they insist that they 'would do anything for a bit of Gold Seal' – loosely translated as a preparedness to contribute a few Silk Cut when Jeremy's rolling the spliff – NOT any sort of inclination to head for the fish bar in Kilburn and score the gear themselves.

During schooltime this crowd ambles lethargically about (its Mecca is the art room) speaking very slowly and deeply to advertise the fact that its collective brain is melting from all the wicked material being pumped into it, and impress-ing the year below with its command of reggae slang.

I cannot deny that I have dabbled occasionally in these murky waters. I am on rather shaky ground here – if you will excuse my continual use of strange geographical meta-phor – since I do not wish to involve anyone in a parental dispute. I can truthfully say that on the majority of occa-sions when I have committed this wicked sin, my close friends have not even been in the vicinity.

What gets me is the fuss everyone makes about it. I don't know what's worse – girls that are sure they will be clapped in jail for going near it or parents who are shocked and terrified by it. I'm not too sure what the basis for parental objection is, so I have consulted my parents (who can't pretend they never saw a spliff in the sixties). Apparently, some people think that marijuana leads to hard drugs. Yeah sure, and using cutlery leads to homicidal knife attacks.

Then my mother suggested that it leads to lack of motivation. I think this is because she has seen people who do nothing but lie around and smoke gear. Well, of course, if you are the type who spends your whole time lying about doing nothing, then what better way to spend the time than smoking spliffs? But it's that way round.

Most of all, it's *boring* when parents of a normal healthy sixteen-year-old girl, who has a couple of spliffs in the same spirit as a couple of glasses of wine when she's out, can't be told about it because they'll assume she's some useless addicted druggie who's throwing her life away. What a lot of fuss about a pleasant harmless activity. I'm sure most of the parents who 'must never find out' have smoked gear in their time and if they haven't, it's about time they started. I don't see how anyone can argue that cigarettes should be legal but spliffs not.

Who would get addicted at those prices anyway? If you're paying around £13 for ⅛ of an ounce – plus bus fares on your way to score – few can be bothered to indulge regularly. Especially since you find yourself scoring a nice little supply and then sharing it with forty uninvited people who get about a toke each. (Interestingly, there are those who can become stoned under these conditions. Even more interestingly, there are those who appear never to inhale at all, but are out of their heads within seconds. That is the magic of the stuff).

Of course, if you think rolling a spliff puts you in danger of missing out, or if no one is prepared to risk their reputation by rolling, you can always cook it. I'll be bringing out the recipe book in time for Christmas.

I remember trying to cook pot flapjacks in a free house once. Not a 'Skunks' Head & Scissors' type of free house, a parent-free house. When parents go away, that spellbinding phrase whizzes round the school as quickly as a bus inspector when your Travelcard's out of date.

We had a list of necessary ingredients – oats, golden syrup, self-raising flour, butter and the Obvious Vital Ingredient, but unfortunately we had to make do with Alpen, honey, cornflour and Stork S.B. (but we bunged in plenty of the O.V.I.)

Not surprisingly, after two hours in the oven our creation was a greyish puddle which we attacked with soup spoons. Yet it produced delightfully genuine effects. I lay on the carpet for a good few hours, realised a great truth about myself (that I was Alice in Wonderland) and returned home in time for my father's birthday breakfast the next day.

Everyone else who was staying the night kept eating well into the small hours, and then turned up at the school swimming sports the next day and pretended they were just in a good mood.

For those who like a moral in the tale, by the way, the following morning my head was like a burglar alarm with no key-holder. I spent my father's birthday breakfast lying on the floor by the dining-room table, and we didn't win the swimming sports either.

But enough of our forays into the phantasmagorical underworld, and onto the other social factions.

There are the Nightclubbers. You've seen them in *The Sun*. They sport little black dresses (which most people would call belts) and trendy hats to trick their way past doormen at Paramount City and The Limelight. They have thirty-five-year-old boyfriends and they don't smoke. You may wonder why they let themselves be photographed by the gutter press with one hand raising the mini-skirt a few inches and the other clutching a bottle of beer. I can enlighten you. It tends to be that they have worn suspenders all evening, uncomfortable little razor-sharp blighters that they are, just in case a thirty-five-year-old hand wanted to creep up the skirt. When there are no advances on the romantic front, they feel that *someone* should appreciate the pain they have suffered on the altar of fashion, so they show off their vogueish accessories to the passing snap-shooters. Simpler than you thought, eh?

Of course, there is a third very upper-middle class sect in whose company we all feel suitably humble. They pool Badminton tickets and meet at the Chelsea Flower Show. They think that the unemployed should clean the streets for their dole money. They go to Balls.

I went to a Gatecrasher Ball once, with the emphasis on the *once*. Journalistic curiosity can justify *one* visit – you can visit South Africa *once*.

Gatecrashers are famous for being the adolescent Sloane's delight – a room full of well-dressed young Ruperts and Harrys hoping for a quick grope on the stroke of midnight (or a quick stroke on the grope of midnight, you never can tell). They are the notorious £16-a-ticket orgies for the upper-middle class teens that give 'peer pressure' a whole new meaning. Not quite my scene, but on a Monday night when I should be revising I'll go anywhere.

Thanks to the scandal-sheets, the Gatecrasher has become a British Institution. Ever since the antics of the well-at-heel teenager were first photographed for *The Sun*, the annual earnings of Gatecrasher entrepreneurs Eddie Davenport and Jeremy Taylor have been public information.

Parents greet any mention of the Balls with fear – tightly gripping their daughter's hand so no one else can grip the rest of her – but, in fact, most teenagers dismiss them with a derisive laugh. They are *not* cool places to hang out.

I was determined that the Heartbeat Ball at the Hammersmith Palais (sorry, *Le* Palais) was not going to shock me. I was well prepared to face a seething mass of naked bodies – quite looking forward to it, in fact.

At first my preconceptions seemed fulfilled. In the pub beforehand there was a wonderful crowd of public school-boys dressed for the Ball, talking about drugs with the noisy abandon of complete amateurs. ('I had a joint in my pocket the other day and the pigs searched me in their van, but they *didn't* find it. By the end they were calling me Sir!')

I'm sure they were, Sir.

So the style of person was not at odds with my presuppositions – now for the Roman orgy.

But what a disappointment it turned out to be! Here was a perfectly normal room full of young dorks in black tie, chatting gently and drinking moderately. As the evening wore on a few manicured hands made polite forays into silk stockings, but no more fervently than at any other teenage parties.

Also, it seemed that most of the people I got talking to were not at all the Gatecrasher stereotypes. I was chatted up by a thirty-year-old haulage contractor named Doug with lines like, 'Are you French? The French are the most beautiful women in the world.' He came to the Ball because, 'there are loads of women here', although I doubt that he was a fifteen-year-old Sloane's dream lover.

Later, we got chatting to a couple of printers from Tooting who had broken through the Gatecrasher's icy élitism by taking the address from an advertisement they had printed. Gatecrashers with a small 'g', I suppose.

This pair honestly wanted to mix with the awful Gatecrasher mob because they planned to send their own kids to public school and wanted to see what they were letting them in for.

One of them asked a girl in the cloakroom queue, in his resonant South London tones, to hand in his ticket for him, and *still* hoped his kids would grow up like her when she turned up her nose with disdain and said, 'I'm tairbly sorry, but I'm in a frateful hurry you see'.

I came to the conclusion that those who look at the Gatecrasher Balls with fear for the sexual morals of the young generation, are worrying unnecessarily. Only one or two ballgoers were getting up to the sort of small thrills reported in papers, and what was much more contemptible than their physical conduct was their almost xenophobic reaction towards mixing with the 'lower classes'.

Besides, it's schools like *mine* that are meant to have a large Gatecrasher following and since I have met, in my entire sixteen years, perhaps *two* people that thought Gatecrasher Balls should be taken seriously, I don't think there is much to worry about.

Most people at school, of course, don't fall so neatly into a social grouping. My social life tends to vary immensely depending on my mood. Most Saturday nights I am too drained from the exertions of the week to go anywhere more strenuous than the pub or the cinema. Every so often we go for a rave, but I try to avoid Paramount City and Gatecrashers like the Plague. Not that I take many steps to avoid the Plague, mind you.

I like parties in people's houses best. That way you can always find somewhere to escape the thumping music, and if you're lucky, talk to people. I do like to think that at sixteen we have outgrown the time when everywhere people went, they hoped to 'get off with someone'. That can be an incredible hassle. Just when you think you're having a nice little conversation, it turns out that from their angle it was only a lead-in to a grope. Then, of course, you (usually) have to think of some sort of excuse that doesn't totally put them off you forever, like you're, 'just getting over a painful relationship'.

I hate the word 'relationship.' If there's one thing I find it incredibly difficult to talk about, it's relationships and deep feelings about people. This is more of a problem than you might think, because most of the people I know love to 'talk relationships through'. I can't stand it.

In the past couple of weeks I have encountered this problem three times. A boy, let us call him Fred, whom I had met at a party the Saturday night before and, shall we say, got to know, telephoned me with the sole purpose of asking me how I felt about him. It was murder. I was lying on my bed, twisting with embarrassment, eating the telephone wire, screwing up my eyes and pulling the tail off my toy pig with mortification at having to tell Fred that I liked him.

Later in the week, for some odd reason, I felt the urge to tell my best friend that she was my best friend. Now Jess is poised, beautiful, mature, sophisticated, universally loved and never has any trouble saying anything. Plus she knows perfectly well that she is my best friend. Yet, in the middle of a private study lesson, I found myself trying to confirm the fact – too embarrassed to say it outright, too embarrassed to write it down, wishing I had never started to speak in the first place.

Eventually I managed to stutter in a small voice: 'Jess, you know, you're like, well, it's sort of that, I feel, I just wanted to say, you see, you're my . . . my . . . my best friend and everything.'

'Is that all?' she asked, getting back down to Moderato Cantabile.

Jess wants to be a psychotherapist, you see, so she's very into openness and verbalising of feelings. I try to oblige, but it just doesn't suit me.

And if you thought it was strange not to be able to tell a 'romance' that I liked him and a best friend that she was a best friend, it has just taken me half an hour to tell my mother that I think she's a really good mother. I don't know what's wrong with me – it's not as though she's about to laugh in my face.

But sixteen and seventeen-year-olds it seems are supposed to like to discuss feelings and relationships, so I guess I'd better pick up the technique.

It didn't work out with Fred, by the way. A week after

our encounter, I was on the bus with Jess and her boyfriend when the boyfriend whispered, 'Look at that complete nork over there.' I turned round and – guess what! Hi Fred, kiss kiss, how are you?

Then we were at a party the next Saturday when another friend said to me, 'Don't look round, but dancing behind you is the completest prat I have ever seen.'

Turning round with an inexplicable sense of foreboding, I found myself confronted – yet again – with Fred. So it had to be goodbye. What a waste of telling him I liked him; it'll probably be several years before I pluck up the nerve to say that to anyone else.

When I'm not embarrassing myself via encounters at parties, or vegging at cinemas/pubs, another place we sometimes patronise is the Bar Escoba in South Kensington.

We were first introduced to it by Soraya, who is Spanish, as is Escoba. We thought we'd humour her in her nostalgia for the Old Country and we went down there one time. We were hooked! Never has there been a place where we have been picked up so often by such varied people. It's wonderful for role-playing and keeping on your toes.

Typical scenario: small moustached man approaches from behind huge grin.

SMALL MOUSTACHED MAN: Chello! Are you American?

ME: Sure am.

MOUSTACHE: I thought so. Where are you from?

VICKI: Boston.

MOUSTACHE: What a fantastic coincidence. I have an aunt in Boston. Which part are you from?

VICKI: Um, um, tiny little suburb, weeny in fact. Wouldn't possibly have heard of it.

MOUSTACHE: And what are you doing here?

VICKI: I'm studying Sanskrit at the University of Cricklewood.

MOUSTACHE: What a coincidence! I speak Sanskrit.

VICKI: No no no, I said Sandpits. Children's habits, you know.

MOUSTACHE: Perhaps we could go for a kebab and talk about it?

VICKI: It sounds jolly tempting, but my friends are wait- ing for me. (Returns to friends amid cries of, 'Onto a good thing there Vic', 'Don't let us keep you' etc. etc.)

Sound cruel? Really, it's harmless fun, no one really expects to form serious romances there.

Only once have Jess and I made a serious contact at Escoba – this was with two rather appetising young Spanish boys, training to be electricians. That minor outbreak lasted until Soraya's sister, who got on much better with them than we did, accidentally let slip that we were *not* eighteen-year old college students, but were doing our GCSEs. AAAAaarrgghh, the humiliation! (Soraya's sister has now been going out with one of them for two months).

Of course, it probably depends on your perspective. I mean, here I am very self-satisfiedly stating that we don't form a boundaried social clique but flit about between them, and everyone else at school is probably sitting there saying, 'What! Don't belong to a clique! That lot who spend all their time either sitting about in the caff or guzzling alcohol like they've been in the desert for a decade?', or however else we are perceived.

And of course, there is interaction between all the differ- ent groups since every so often we realise that, despite being totally different, we can enjoy each other's company. As long as it only happens occasionally, it can be great fun when everyone from school goes to the same party and there we all are – dancing clique-to-clique.

6 | The Old Folks at Home

Problems with Parents

What is wrong with my parents could, naturally, fill a book itself.

No normal child can go through life without periods of immense irritation with parents. When I was about fourteen, everything they ever did or said irritated me. I think that phase is past now, but every so often I have a little recurrent bout.

Some days I am in the mood to be a good daughter, so I bounce about being affectionate and helpful. (I don't recognise this, think my parents, leafing through). Some days I just lurk in a corner, waiting to make an argument out of something one of them has said. Some days I feel really guilty because I can't display affection. They might hold out their arms for a hug and I will just leave the room. Sometimes they want to be kissed goodnight and I physically can't manage to do it. Not always – on days when I can show affection, I overdo it so I have some in stock for the next day. No wonder they get puzzled.

What most parents seem to feel the lack of is emotional input. When they say, as they really do, 'This house is not a hotel,' it is often not referring to their kid's habit of dumping its clothes in the washing basket and demanding that its food is put in front of it immediately, but to its lack of overt signs of love. The idea seems to be that a normal loving child can't stand to see its mother staggering about under piles of clothes and slaving over a hot stove – it feels a real *want* to help in the house, visit its great-great-aunt, cook the occasional meal . . . They don't seem to accept for an argument that their kid is just a nasty person who doesn't feel these desires.

Sometimes they really think their child doesn't love them enough.

'You're not a part of this family,' some of them say, 'You never want to spend time with us. You were such a loving little girl.'

The you-were-an-amazing-two-year-old ploy is my least favourite. I was, it seems, an impeccable toddler. Apparently I loved tidiness and I was forever straightening up my room. I was very caring and affectionate, I loved to play let's-help-mother. None of this is in my memory banks.

As I have said before, my friends think (or say they think) my parents are pretty reasonable, due to the fact that they are quite sensible about letting me out until a decent hour and not forbidding me from staying out for the night etc.

I can never decide what I *want* my friends to think of my parents. Some days it's nice to think their leniency is enviable. Some days, when I am angry with them and want to have a good bitch, the last thing I want to hear is some friend saying, 'Well, they're better than *my* parents, I wouldn't mind having them.'

Naturally, you'd have to be a bit strange to tell your friends all about your parents' good qualities and how you really love them and care for them. Yet whenever you have a massive row and think that your parents are, in fact, the most unreasonable, violent-tempered, deliberately annoying people in the Western World, who do you tell about it?

Your best friend. So friends tend to get a bit of a warped view of a parent's true nature. When they like them in spite of it, it's very worrying. I mean, from what I tell my friends you would think that my parents do nothing but shout at me, beat me up, enslave me in the kitchen and openly prefer my brother. Yet they still say, 'I really like your dad – and your mum's so sweet.' Can't understand it. But it's the same the other way round, of course. My friends' parents seem incredibly nice and relaxed, infinitely preferable to mine on many counts, but as soon as I am out of the way Mr and Mrs Hyde sneak out and inflict evil tortures on their helpless children.

My parents hate to think that I tell tales on them to my friends. Sometimes if I am particularly angry, I might ring Jess in front of them and start saying, 'Jesus, my parents are so disgusting, you would not believe what they just did . . .' and then leave the room, enigmatically, with the phone.

But I know they do exactly the same thing. If I'm going out on a Saturday night, I tend to meet their friends just coming in. It's all very amicable and we like each other (I *think*), but I'm sure that, the minute I'm out of the house, my mother will start telling them all about how Giles and I are useless and unmanageable, what should she do, etc. etc.

Luckily, they have grown out of their little phase of comparing us unfavourably to other peoples' children. They always deny that they did this, but we know it's true. When we were in prep school they would seriously say things like, 'Apparently Ned is going to the library every day in the holidays, why can't you?' and 'Alice made some lovely little cakes for her mother's party – you never do anything like that.'

One of my strongest memories is of being unable to finish a piece of meat and being told by my father that, 'Philip always finishes what's on his plate.' I mean, for goodness' sake! How could he know something like that? Either he's bluffing, or he and his friends have some exceedingly boring conversations.

Then there's the terrible Krypton Factor challenge of getting the parents through the School Meeting. I have weasled out of a good few of them by forgetting to tell my parents they were happening until too late, or simply by forging negative replies to send to school.

School meetings are odd, since they form an intersection of my two lives. 'I can't believe you behave like this at school,' my parents often say to me. They don't realise quite how different a person I am when I'm at school. There I like to think I'm a relatively easy-going person. When I'm with my friends, that is. I'm absolute hell to teach – annoying, talkative, distracting, impertinent. I get angry with them for telling me off, but secretly I don't understand why they agree to carry on teaching me. I'd just throw me out.

So anyway, I like to think I'm quite easy-going when I'm with my friends, I don't pick arguments and shout at them and refuse to be affectionate like I do at home. I've tried to explain it to my parents but they just say, 'Well, be like that at home then,' and they really think I'm just the same with my friends but they don't point it out so I don't realise.

Then along they come to a parents' meeting and I'm not sure who I'm supposed to be. Luckily, I'm too busy worrying about the impression they'll be making on each other and the trouble I'll be in when my teachers have spilled the beans about me, to really think about it.

Now I'm old and responsible (i.e. I could leave school if I wanted to), it seems that I'm allowed to be present at the conversation between teacher and parent. Few things in life are worse than standing across the room from where your mother and the Physics teacher are shaking with conspiratorial laughter. You grip your cup of watery tea and stale sponge cake and trying to imagine what is being said.

'Yes, she's *just* like that at home,' you can feel your mother saying.

'Don't be silly, she doesn't really have a skin problem – did she tell you that?' you see your father saying to the games teacher, 'She just swims like a brick.'

As the quarter-of-an-hour winds to a close, you see them taking leave of each other like old friends, then they both look at you and smile secretly.

'What were you talking about?' you ask your mother in the car.

'I can't really remember, darling,' she says, 'Are we on the right road?'

Then again, it can be worse to actually be there. This year I had to suffer through hearing my parents asking embarrassing questions ('Just exactly which Oxford college will she be applying for, do you think?') but it was quite enjoyable watching the teachers want to say all sorts of horrible things, then giving me a nervous glance and deciding not to.

At times like these, I do feel a little school spirit, though. All I want to hear from my parents is how wicked (positive term) they think my teachers are, how beautiful the school is, how handsome my tutor is and so on. I may complain about school, but not a whisper of criticism will I tolerate from Outsiders like my parents. I used to have no school spirit at all but, as I grow old and boring, I'm cultivating a little pride in it. I even allowed my parents to come to the Christmas concert last year – on strict condition that they praised everything and didn't sing. I wasn't involved in the concert, but they dragged me in to find props for the central playlet. All I had to come up with (in two days) was an authentic warrior's sword, eight brown leather belts and a wine bottle dated around 1 AD. They got a piece of wood wrapped in tin foil, two belts (one of them blue, both of them mine) and a water bottle circa 1988. Well, I didn't volunteer for it.

I still don't see why they have the right to come to parents' meetings and get reports though. How would they feel if Giles and I walked around their offices being told their secrets? ('Your mother is quite a dedicated worker, but she *will* pass notes during operations', 'Now, your father is not without a good brain, but if he keeps up this sniggering during board meetings then he will find his work going seriously downhill.')

I mean, school is my haven from parental control – it's where I disappear to in the mornings and materialise back from in the evening. If they're lucky I'll tell them if I've had a good day. Then, suddenly, a report arrives or they go to a meeting and my whole Other Life is laid bare. The characters who inhabit my parents' working worlds are faceless to me – I hear about what goes on, but I never see. My parents can stroll into my classroom and meet the protagonists of my school tales – it's NOT FAIR.

I will not inflict this horror on my own children. (I plan to have six or seven by the way – I watch *The Waltons* a lot). I will not agree to let them read their reports first and then rip them open, pretending I have forgotten the agreement. I will not drive them to forging negative replies to school meeting invitations – I will let them have their privacy.

People bring up their children so weirdly, don't they? I mean, they speak to them in high voices, using strange words (do you actually want your kid to call a train a 'choo-choo'?), giving them odd things to play with . . . if the child grew up the way that seems to be intended, its parents would be a little bemused. The child thinks that if it comes across a large purple dinosaur it should play with it. It wears frilly dresses, boy or girl – society would rather mal-treat a young lad who didn't dispense of that habit pretty sharpish. It is encouraged to play in the park free from all clothing restrictions and, around Christmas each year, it is taken to sit in the lap of a fat bearded man in a red coat it has never met before.

Speaking of speaking, goodness knows how I ever picked it up. When I see my parents talking to other babies, I realise that they clearly didn't introduce proper English to me among the gurgles for a good few years. Not only that, but apparently they used to play me Chinese records when I went to sleep, hoping I would grow up bi-lingual. I know they were young then, but that's ridiculous. My learning to talk normally had the odds stacked rather highly against it.

I speak to all babies and children (mine will, I hope, be no exception) as I would speak to anyone else. Eventually they will be able to reply. Why create more hassles for yourself by letting it get to three and then having to teach it a whole new vocabulary?

My parents also, it seems, considered sending me to the French Lycée, but decided against it. Blast them, what a useful definite A-level that would have been. Look at all the trouble I'm going to to learn French, when I could have just soaked it up easily. I'd like to send my children there, but I don't think I'll be privately educating seven children. If I had twenty-five thousand a year to spare, you don't think I'd be frittering it away on thankless offspring do you? If I'm going to be a poverty-stricken authoress, starving for her art in a garret in the Scottish Highlands, I won't be doling out the thousands hither and thither. Besides, I want my kids to have all the disadvantages I never had.

A year ago, or when I was fifteen, I wrote: 'Parents are odd creatures. They fork out incredible sums for a couple of quails' eggs and a bottle of Chablis, when you can get a deep-pan pizza, toppings of your choice, extra cheese and a glass of Coke for a fiver. When do you stop wanting junk food and start wanting everything in miniscule helpings with creamy sauce? And why?' Parents seemed like a different species. Now I occasionally catch myself seeing their point of view – I'll take the Chablis if not the quail's eggs.

I worry about these wider sympathies – they mean I'm getting older.

The closest I've come to parenthood so far is adoptive parenthood. A couple of years ago, bored with socks and brilliantine, I decided to give my father something interesting for his birthday so I flicked through the catalogue of animals available for adoption at London Zoo. I really wanted a toucan, but they were all taken. Most of the appealing or funny animals go quickly and if you don't move fast you're stuck with a tree toad or a stick insect. I chose a pelican.

A couple of months after the birthday we decided to pay our new little son a visit. There was meant to be a plaque with my father's name on it by his cage, but unfortunately the plaque had *my* name on it and was in the secretary's office for security reasons. Not because the men of Britain were rushing to get their hands on a momento of me, but because it kept being vandalised. Nothing personal, we were assured.

I had not foreseen the problems with being a parent. We worried for the little lad's welfare. We asked if it was getting enough to eat, whether it had everything it needed. Perhaps it would like a toaster in its room.

But it was silent. I had expected it to be bubbling over with enthusiasm about life in general, but it looked wordlessly into the distance. Ashamed of its mother already.

My father, having put one son through boarding school before, was used to this sort of thing. Come on, he said. He's embarrassed to be emotional in front of the other pelicans, he has to live with them you know. Just blow a kiss and let's go.

This was not good enough for me. How was I to know the little fellow was not unhappy? I thought of smuggling a file into its lunchtime haddock.

I looked at the other plaques, wondering idly whether Coca-Cola had this trouble with Dilberta the elephant, or the Waitrose Social Club with its boa constrictor. (Bloody good symbol for a social club, a boa constrictor. I bet the Waitrose has a long waiting list).

Eventually I waved to our little pelican and we left it, surrounded by its friends. In the car we discussed the best time to tell it it was adopted.

So you see, my one attempt at motherhood was not that successful. Maybe it would work better with a real baby, but I'm not so sure. Whenever I baby-sit for my little cousin Max, I start off by speaking to him with normal adult respect but eventually, unable to stop him crying, I bounce little green pigs in front of him and sing, 'What's this, Maxy? What's this, hmmm?' in a high voice, trying desperately to cheer him up. Just what my parents always think will happen to other areas of my life – when it comes to reality, all principle goes out the window.

But just wait till I have seven children reading Dickens while still in nappies. I'll prove my system yet.

7 | Home Groan

The Problems of Traditional Family Life

No family is happy all the time – except perhaps that of my friend Kate, whose parents seem limitlessly understanding and affectionate, whose sister is *never* patronising or unfriendly and over whose house reigns an air of shameless felicity.

Of course, you can never be completely sure what anybody else's home life is really like – as proved by the fact that several people (who do not know Kate) have told me that mine is the happiest family they know. Ha! True, we all manage to make it to the dinner table at the same time on a regular basis, we don't hate to be together, there is no shadow of marital break-up, but we argue all the time – *all* the time. We rather enjoy it, in fact. My brother arrived home from university for the Christmas holidays and over his welcome-home meal we had a satisfying row over who was talking the most. 'I've missed this,' said Giles, 'At university meals, nobody ever shouts, "You've ruined my dinner!" and runs out crying.'

We have intellectual arguments, when my father will say, 'Well, unless you've read (names some tome of which I've never heard) then you really can't comment', upon which the real meat of the row will become the right to offer opinion and not the original subject. We have emotional arguments, when we make personal remarks about each other and take back any affectionate comments we have ever made. We have Guilt Trip arguments, when we all remind each other what we have done for each other, and swear never to accept familial favours again.

There are a few favourite topics for argument. The TV is a perfect source. My father can never understand How On Earth I Can Possibly Watch *Blind Date* and *Neighbours*, and is usually arguing the case for switching to a heartstoppingly boring documentary about planes, during which he can point excitedly to the screen and say, 'Look, it's a real Mark II Spitfire, look at it Toria, look.'

'Yeah.'

School is another good provoker. Some days my mother is much too interested in what goes on and I shout at her – some days she isn't interested enough and I shout at her. I'm a real joy to have around the house.

There is one major stumbling block in the way of perfect parent-child relations in our house, and that is the rôle of the relationship. The Corens of yesteryear, you see, treated their parents with respect, courtesy and heartfelt gratitude for having been brought in to the world. What do I do? Wander about with my hand outstretched for more money, refusing to go out unless I get a lift, never opening my mouth unless it's to criticise. Ah yes, times have changed since the days when my grandmother walked down to the corner shop leaving the front door gaping open, bought all the food for the next month and still had change out of a hen.

Nowadays children are expected to confide their problems and chat informally about their lives, and it is very confusing for us modern children to see our parents treating us like friends, waiting for us to relax and treat *them* as equals so they can shriek, 'I never spoke to my parents like that!'

The traditional ideals of family life are appealing at a distance, but they rarely work out so well in practice. Until I was fourteen, we had a cottage in the New Forest. Naturally I have rose-coloured memories of the place; just as summer always seems golden in retrospect, country cottages seem magical. In sentimental moments I think back to long walks through dappled woods, horses trotting past the front gate, the merry brook at the bottom of the garden and crumpets and Monopoly by the fire.

Some of this actually went on, of course, but there was another side to it. There was the occasional sun-dappled walk, but huddling indoors moaning about the lack of central heating and the rising damp while the weather grizzled against the window was far more usual. Horses trotting past the front gate; well, more often they trotted *through* the front gate trampling the flowerbeds. As for wildlife in general I was terrified of the cows that hung about on street corners like something out of *West Side Story*. The bedroom I shared with my brother was hardly a contented nest as I couldn't stand the things that flew and he couldn't stand the things that scuttled.

The merry brook at the bottom of the garden, when I dared to dash through the horse-filled paddock to get to it, was merry enough as brooks go, but I got very used to that sudden feeling of pressure against the top of your gumboots just before the tide slops over and soaks your socks. This left me too soggy to run back through the paddock, and as there was no way I was going to brave the 'wild' horses, I tended to sit and cry until someone came to get me. In the final years the brook lost its merriness anyway; a certain *je ne sais quoi* disappeared the day a local farmer started dumping washing machines into it and calling them a rockery.

Crumpets and Monopoly in front of the fire? Well it didn't take too long for us to get a TV set and after that, believe me, the rural life went out of the window. We discovered that if our parents chainsmoked very quickly, and we hung grey paper from the walls and glued our eyes to the box, we could fool ourselves into believing we were still in London. Then we would be perfectly content until a splash of water fell from the roof and a spider came racing across the floor to remind us that this was the forest after all.

The problem was, much as we enjoyed the cottage when we were younger (there is a time, albeit brief, when a kid likes getting wet and falling in cowpats and sleeping with creepy-crawlies and running about in a glorious mud-coated daze) we outgrew it fairly soon. As the greasy, spot-covered, depressed figure of teenagehood beckoned and the bunk beds groaned as we climbed on, and we groaned when we rolled on to the Winchester bypass, we knew that the good old days were over. Sometimes we were forced to invent plays and parties and sports matches as an excuse not to get out the freezer box and head south-west.

I remember packing giant weekend suitcases of magazines, make-up (one has to be optimistic, even in the country), Sony walkmen (to shut out the birdsong), blindfolds (so we wouldn't have to watch the parents donning brown corduroy flares to weed the garden), address books (yes, Dad, that was me running up a huge phone bill to keep in touch with London), mosquito nets (don't tell me that the spider is just as scared of me; I have always hated the eight-legged little blighters and I always will), and money.

Why money? I hear you cry. What is there to buy in the New Forest except eggs from the annual passing salesman? Well, here was another factor to mark my change in development. I had caught that serious early-teenage bug of wanting to spend money on silly things. When my father was going down to Sandy Balls (yes, go ahead, laugh, get it out of your system) to fetch the papers, it was not unheard of for me to have a crying fit if denied the privilege of going with him to buy a magazine or some chocolate. I made them take me to Fordingbridge every Saturday so I could stroll around town lightening the jingle in my pockets. Stuff the peaceful wooded walks, said my thirteen-year-old self, show me some action. And of course fairly soon even walking around the Co-op in Fordingbridge wasn't action enough, and that's when it was time to sell up and move back to Cricklewood.

Physically leaving the cottage was a wrench. Seeing its heartstring potential ('You sold the cottage, the least you could do is buy me a stereo') I perhaps slightly overplayed the distressed valedictorian. Yet I *was* very sad to lose it, mainly because the letting go of the cottage was a tangible sign of growing up and change, but also because there *were* a few golden walks in the woods, horses trotting past the gate and games of Monopoly in front of the fire, and you don't get much of that in Cricklewood.

Besides, now I'm sixteen I'm into my second childhood – all that spending money and listening to Walkmen is a thing of the past. And I've always been obsessed by games – not just Monopoly. I spent 87 per cent of my formative years trying to blackmail my family into playing various board games with me. Cluedo was a favourite – as long as I was allowed to be Professor Plum. You won't catch *me* being gormless old Reverend Green.

I like to buy people games for Christmas, you can always go and buy those nice new ones with titles like 'Over The Hill', 'Midlife Crisis' etc. with which to insult your parents. But I have to admit that they're always terrible. Nothing is ever as good as the proper old games.

Although I suppose Trivial Pursuit is quite good, and that's newish. I went through a phase of manic Trivial Pursuit playing while I was taking my GCSEs, and I soon found that the style of questions was hardly different. ('How many fingers had Anne Boleyn?', What was the relevance of the pointing-bone in prehistoric medicine?'. Which one is from Trivial Pursuits, which from the GCSE paper?

But I cracked the system, and then the game lost its challenge. I soon found that the answer to the sports questions is, nine times out of ten, Muhammad Ali or Red Rum. For History it's Henry VIII; Geography, the Magellan Straits; Science and Nature, an apiary; Art and Literature, Van Gogh's other ear or Mr Micawber.

Pets are another feature of traditional family life. I have never been lucky with pets. We only had a cat because half its tail had fallen off and its owners didn't want it. We hung onto it for six years, during which time it was beaten up every day by the cat next door before finally dying of the cat 'flu.

Fish are a joke. Every so often I go out and buy ten lovely fan-tailed fish, nine of which die over the following week and the tenth lives for seven years despite fervent attempts to kill it off to pave the way for more. My father, on the other hand, can win a cheapo midget fish from Hampstead fair, lob it in the garden pond, forget to feed it, let the pond freeze over, and the blasted thing survives every time. My satisfaction comes from watching him buy tadpoles which never turn into frogs. I don't know how he does it, but he always ends up with a bowlful of tadpoles as big as hand grenades.

The pet with which I built up the best rapport was my hamster. I bought him way back when I was nine. There was a hamster craze on. There were always crazes at prep school. There was a sticker craze — our classroom was like a Turkish market as we sat round with handfuls of stickers crying out, 'A Scratch 'n' Sniff banana for this Oily? Are you mad! You can only get them in the Peruvian jungle if you're related to the tribal king and know the password. It deserves four holograms and a Garfield at *least*!' There was a multi-entrance pencil case craze. People were coming in with nine-door pencil cases and being treated like pariahs by those commanding twelve doors. There was a smelly pencil craze, until they were banned by the headmistress.

I felt particularly left out the day Jessica had her ears pierced. Jess was a bit of a trendsetter at prep school, and the day she came in with little red-and-gold earrings marked the beginning of a new era. Earrings swept across the classroom like insects. Long hair and a deep-rooted terror of pain kept my ears naked, however, and I greedily awaited the next trend. The day that ears went out and rodents came in, I galloped to Harrods for the first small whiskered thing I could get my hands on. That is how my relationship with Sebastian began.

Sebastian was always coming down with something. He arrived perfectly healthy, but turned into a sort of furry grandmother who was always bedding-ridden with colds or sore feet or a skin problem. We spent half our time bathing him in chemicals and putting medicine in his water bottle. I decided that this was because he was a very rare and superior hamster, and every time we saw the vet I went proudly into school and sniggered at those with common healthy hamsters.

Jessica's hamster, predictably, died first. Poor little Milly, he could no longer take the shame of having a girl's name and he fell ill. There was no cure, and Jess's father was forced to put little Milly out of his misery by stuffing him into a milk bottle. Mirroring their owners' fashion-consciousness, the other hamsters followed suit. Joanna came home from holiday to find that Houdini had been

buried by the builder. Becky's hamster Quaver was next –
I'm not sure quite what happened, but I always suspected
them of maltreatment.

Sebastian himself was finally killed off by 'flu while staying with the vet. I raced to the surgery, but too late – he
had already been cremated. It took years to get over the
grief, and I insisted that his cage was kept exactly as he left
it.

I'll say this for my family – they were very supportive
through that terrible time. My mother had battled with her
severe rodentaphobia to help me give him his little baths,
and they were both very understanding after his passing.
My brother made hamster jokes for a month.

So you see, we are the perfect family after all.

8 | A Fat Lot of Help

Problems with Nannies and Home Helps

Welcoming a stranger into your home is not a safe exercise. I mean, it's hard enough trying to get along with your family.

When I was small, I had nannies. One main one and a few little ones here and there. That is to say, from three till eight I had Vivienne as a surrogate mother. Before and after her stay with us, we couldn't keep hold of anyone for more than a few weeks.

I don't remember very clearly the helps before Vivienne, except for one or two. There was Julie, who was great and one of the few pre-Vivienne nannies who left still friends with us and kept in touch for years afterward. My brother also had a great nanny, who left after I turned up and spoilt things.

I remember one help who kept about thirteen budgies in her room, in a cage about three inches square. She was smoked out. One girl stayed with us for literally a day – upon which she took us swimming. Finding I needed to go to the lavatory, I asked her to take me. She instructed me just to use the pool. I marched straight to my mother and demanded her immediate dismissal. One girl was found raiding the fridge in the night by my father, and was so embarrassed that she resigned on the spot. Can't think why - I am often found raiding the fridge in the night by my father. I just shout at him till he goes away.

Then, of course, Vivienne reigned for five glorious years. She was the perfect nanny: strict, no-nonsense, practical and Welsh. Funny to think that when she first arrived she was only seventeen (a child!) but to me she seemed unbelievably old. Giles and I were terrified of her, much more so than we were of my parents. The only naughtiness we ever got up to was on a Tuesday – Vivie's night off. We used to have 'Fun Nights' – which involved trying to guess what our parents' dinner guests would be wearing and peering through the banisters to see if we were right, and then playing three-and-in with a sponge football. *And* we could brush our teeth without Vivie giving us marks out of five and sending us back to do it again if we got anything less than three.

It was a very up-and-down relationship, like any parent-child one, but the only time I remember feeling any real animosity towards Vivie was when she spanked the cat for relieving itself on her twenty-first birthday cards. I realise now that it wasn't very gentlemanly of Percy.

Once she took us back to visit her family in Wales, which was the first time we've ever been anywhere without our parents. I seem to remember getting engaged to her little brother – I wonder if that still stands? I rather liked the idea of being engaged, and I told everyone at school about it. I didn't let on that it wasn't a *real* engagement, and everybody thought I was well cool. It's probably the only reason why Jess is still friends with me today – secret awe. I remember the day I came in and told her that I had decided to terminate the engagement. 'I feel free,' I remember saying – I was only about nine. I told all sorts of dreadful lies at prep school. I remember telling one girl in my class that I was really a boy but, as my parents already had one of those, they dressed me in skirts and pretended I was a girl. I even said, in a very deep voice (or so I thought), 'This is my real voice, but I have to disguise it normally.' I didn't realise that an eight-year old boy's voice would probably be higher than mine, not vice versa.

I did long to be a boy when I was little. I was the definitive tomboy, most people assumed I was a boy. I had short hair and I wore trousers at every possible opportunity. I went around with a fellow gender-bender called Holly, except that we didn't refer to ourselves as Holly and Vicki. Certainly not indeed. We went through a whole series of different names, the most longstanding being George and Timmy after a couple of characters from *The Famous Five*. God knows what I was doing being Timmy the dog, for goodness' sake. I used to catch sticks, all sorts of things.

Then we were Oliver and the Artful Dodger, and went through a serious Oliver Twist phase. We even convinced the school to put it on as a play – with Holly playing Oliver and me as Dodger of course. I was ill on the night and someone else played him. That's probably why I'm not an actress to this day.

All this role-playing was a little confusing. Some days I wasn't sure whether I was Dodger or Timmy. I remember staying the night at Holly's house and eating a bowl of gruel on all fours. And you thought kids were normal till puberty.

So anyway, I went to Wales and got engaged to Vivienne's brother - with whom I fell madly in love after he removed a huge spider from the bathroom. It didn't take much in those days. Still doesn't, actually.

Of course, eventually the time came for Vivienne to leave. 'You can laugh or cry, whichever you like,' she told us. I cried. Giles roared with laughter. We always were incompatible.

We begged her to stay, our parents got a really hard time as we thought it was all their fault. They were on a massive guilt trip anyway, as they thought we considered Vivie our mother/parents and we didn't know them, and maybe we shouldn't have had a nanny. There was something in that. We did know our parents, they weren't the really bad neglectful type who left us all to the nanny, of course we loved them and saw them a lot and all that, but naturally since we spent three-quarters of our time with Vivie she was bound to be of major importance. I thought I wouldn't be able to cope with her not being there but, of course, we adjusted pretty quickly, we wrote letters and she visited and eventually our parents took over. But I still think about her, and certain things remind me of her – like all the other things from childhood that are stored away somewhere. You can't play in the sprinkler all your life.

After Vivie, I don't think my parents wanted another major mother figure, so we went for the mother's help type. For the past five years, we had been sniggering quietly at all those families who couldn't hang on to their home helps while we had Vivienne. The laugh was now on the other foot. Home helps came and went like . . . like buses, I was going to say, but that implies that we had four at a time and then none for months. Anyway, they came and went like something that comes and goes a lot.

There was a girl from Essex whose speech Giles and I began subconsciously to imitate. That was a period of total breakdown of parental relations. My mother tried to teach me to speak 'properly' again, and I still tense up just thinking about it. It's a shame she didn't stay longer, I might have had a normal speaking voice now, instead of this appalling posh one that gets me into fights, and no wonder.

One lady came for a while as a mother's help, but she

was really a ship's cook. She insisted on wearing a black-and-white uniform and a cap, she served dinner to us in the dining room on silver plates with lots off tiny potatoes to garnish it and she *always* picked up the phone and said, 'Mr Corrigan's residence.' I have to admit I teased her a little – just as my mother had convinced her that our name was 'Coren', she would get it right on the phone and I would say, 'No no, it's Corrigan.' Nice of me, eh? She was very proprietorial over the kitchen – if one of us wanted so much as an omelette, she would insist on making it. She was very sweet and motherly, but we're slobs at heart and we couldn't take the high life for long. Out she went. Actually, I think she resigned after buying some mushrooms that my mother thought looked tired. It wasn't really any of my mother's business, it seemed.

Then we had Isabelle from France for a while – my parents took over as surrogate mother and father to her. I remember them giving her some pocket money for a trip to Shakespeare's Birthplace. I was very jealous. I don't know what happened to her, but I do remember one embarrassing night when everyone was out except for the two of us and, on hearing a noise downstairs, she insisted that we called the police. Eleven of them swarmed over the house with torches but there was nothing there. I told my parents that the police reckoned he might have slipped out of the back when they arrived, but I think they suspected the truth. I know it's meant to be good to phone the police, even if it's only a slight chance, but it's taken me a good few years to get over the embarrassment of that one.

Who knows to what extent the law is preventative medicine? We have a policeman coming to school every year to tell us about self-defence and stopping yourself getting attacked. The stuff which is easiest to carry out (like looking very positive and confident as you walk along) is the stuff that seems least sound practically speaking. I mean, how do you know that there isn't a rapist lurking about who hates women and is, in fact, angered still further by the sight of some girl swaggering along looking tough? Maybe a little gentle pleading would do better.

I am prepared to take a few steps to try and keep myself relatively safe from attack, beyond which I will not go. All right, I won't walk home alone across Battersea at four in the morning, I won't open the door and invite a strange man with a bulky carrier bag into the house when there's nobody home, but I am not prepared to stop going out at night and look dowdy and greasy to prevent sexual assault and keep one hand attached to a fly-spray at all times – when I look dowdy and greasy, its wholly accidental. It seems that so many people are wasting the benefit of not being attacked by spending their whole lives worrying that they will be. I mean, if you're only ever going to go out in broad daylight, and only then to walk down a crowded high street, well armed and underdressed, then what's the point of never having been attacked – you're behaving as if you have been.

Why my parents think I will be safer if I come home at one-thirty rather than two, I don't know. Sometimes I will be at a party in a very safe area, with a nice safe cab booked to bring me back to my nice safe home, but they still insist that I leave earlier than I want to for 'safety reasons' – which are no reasons at all. They tend to argue that they can't go to sleep while I'm still out, but many's the time I've come home early from somewhere brilliant to find them snoring contentedly away, dreaming of anything but what might be happening to their defenceless teenage daughter. Sometimes parents (not mine, but others) seem to think their daughters *want* to be raped and murdered, what with all the rules they lay down. As if we would really put ourselves in situations where we thought we were in real danger.

But all this is detracting somewhat from the home help theme. Where were we? Ah yes, Isabelle and her hoax police calls.

Obviously, between all these diverse women who were actually hired, we had to do a hell of a lot of interviewing. that is, my mother had to do a lot of interviewing, I just sat there and made life difficult. (So what else is new?)

One girl, I have always felt guilty about this, came over for lunch-and-an-interview. She had several A-levels and degrees and things, so we reckoned she was far too intelligent to stick it out with us for long, and we didn't hire her. Some months later when she applied for a similar position with some unbelievably intelligent friends of ours, we said that we had really liked her and thought she'd be a great choice.

She drove off in the family car and never came back.

One lunch-and-interview candidate ate her McDonald's with a knife and fork. She was out.

We gave up eventually. We decided that it wasn't worth all that hassle – we could probably handle cooking, washing-up, washing and ironing, cleaning and shopping among ourselves. It was a wise decision. Now my mother does everything.

9 | Getting Educated

GCSE and Other School Problems

When I was due to leave prep school, back in 1982, all dressed and ready to move onto Big Girls' School, I was officially informed that I was too young to leave, and I was going to stay on for another year. Had I forgotten that I had skipped a year when I first started because I was the only person who could read?

So I spent most of 1983 sitting about in the school library with the other four who had been too young to make the break, not having any lessons, and generally enjoying ourselves. Little did I know what this extra year was going to mean.

Yes, I fell into the GCSE year. Lucky old me, always at the wrong place at the wrong time, managed to get myself trapped into the guinea pig year for the new exam.

In 1986, when our year was told that we were going to be the testing year, we automatically became staunch adversaries of the new exam. Of course we did. Everyone in every year, O-level or A-level, GCSE or just the normal school year, always complains about having too much work, about the teachers being incompetent, about the syllabus being boring. It's normal to complain when you're young. It's normal to complain when you're old.

Anyway, because we were the first year, everyone was on the look-out for complaints. Our parents were worried that we were going to suffer. Our teachers were worried that we were going to worry. The government was worried that it wasn't going to work.

Thus we got the idea that our complaining was justified. It seemed expected of us. So it got louder.

The first piece I wrote about the GCSE in *The Telegraph* was so reactionary that it's embarrassing to read:

> Like all the other guinea pigs for the new exam, I have discovered not only that the books in the school library are going to be of little use since the emphasis is so different, but that my relationship with my teachers could well be what differs most of all.
>
> Continuous assessment is at the heart of the change, and it is not a pleasant feature. It is not simply that instead of two hours of pressure and nerves we are now treated to two years' worth; it is also that our teachers, who were poaching on our side against the O-level examiners, have suddenly turned gamekeeper. . . .
>
> . . . GCSE proponents argue that the examination-based system favoured those who could learn how to store and retrieve knowledge. I would argue that that is what education is all about.

Dearie me! Our teachers have turned gamekeeper? Could that be a hint of paranoia I sense creeping in there?

By June 1988, when I had finished taking the exams whose presence I didn't even seem to recognise in the first piece, I had everything in slightly better perspective:

> We did not stop to see if the new GCSE was actually a major change – which, of course, it isn't: a bit more

coursework, a slightly different, but no less erudite, emphasis . . .

. . . Traditionalists believe that the GCSE generation is being impregnated with a lot of useless 'skills' at the expense of factual learning but, in substance, most syllabuses are barely changed.

. . . As for History, we spent four terms preparing intensively two main subjects – England under Elizabeth I and The History of Medicine – with constant testing of our knowledge and understanding. Any candidate who can convince an examiner in the total absence of that concentrated study that he fully understands the topic set, deserves whatever grade he gets.

It is all very well to guess at the Elizabethan peasant mentality and write your empathetic description of Elizabeth's Government 'from the rustic point of view' in a perfect Gloucester accent, but 90 per cent of the marks will be for the background knowledge incorporated. GCSE is not about abolishing fact, just using it slightly more laterally.

I'm a complete GCSE convert now, although I know that I personally would have been better suited to an O-level paper. I'm not very good at keeping to the same standard all the way across two years, and yet I can see that that is a much fairer system of testing. My results are open to individual interpretation, they are the sort of results which stun some people with their brilliance, disappoint others with their averageness, but cause most people to try and fathom how *I* felt about them before they commit themselves to congratulating or commiserating. Oh all right, four A's, five B's and a C. Not that I would have wanted ten A's (and Neil Kinnock doesn't want to be Prime Minister). It *would* be embarrassing to have too many A's, though, when it comes to exchanging results with friends.

The main thing that I didn't like about GCSE was the modernisation. The system, I now realise, is fine. It's the up-to-dating of the questions that doesn't work. The maths paper was stuffed with questions like, 'How much will the building society loan Harminder Singh, given his £10,000 income?' I liked to be asked whether Martha Mildew or Brenda Big got the larger piece of cake, I never felt the lack of reality to be a problem.

If there's some sort of question about archery in GCSE, you know that the one with the highest score is bound to be the girl. You know that the one who sews the petticoat fastest is bound to be the boy. It's so predictable, it's boring.

But off the subject of GCSE, which I would now like to bury in my past, and onto other school complaints. There are a few subjects which caused me real concern over the years I was taking them, and not just for the sake of griping.

Take music, for instance. Imagine Bernard Manning being slowly strangled – that is the sound of my singing. As I have been made to demonstrate.

Just imagine that, when you get into work today, your colleagues will have arranged their chairs in a neat circle and you will be expected to stand in the middle of them and sing. Alone.

Don't fancy the idea? Well luckily, that sort of thing doesn't happen to adults. It does to children, though. Once a week we used to file into the music hall and fight for the inconspicuous places at the back. I would then spend thirty-five minutes slouched, broken and trembling, in my seat, silently praying not to be chosen to sing. They got me every time.

In the last century, girls would sit down to grand pianos after dinner and enchant their audiences. Nowadays there is no opportunity to show off an entertaining singing voice. It is far more useful to tell a good joke, or make interesting conversation. So why aren't children taught more up-to-date social skills? I would love to learn how to make conversation with someone I had never met before and with whom I had nothing in common. Besides, it isn't possible to teach someone a talent like singing if they aren't born with it. Is it the humiliation that they feel is good for us?

Singing would be an excellent punishment for criminals. Imagine it – someone mugs an old lady and they then had to spend forty-eight hours singing in a public place. That would get the crime rate down pretty sharpish.

Then there's History. If there's one subject that I feel at once innately interested in, yet totally confused by, it is History.

I've never learnt about the Second World War. Now I'm doing my A-levels (English, French, Italian. I'm ready for 1992, are you?) History is in more ways than one, a thing of the past. In other words, I will never learn about the Second World War. Everything I know about it is dredged up from the various TV series and mini-series that I have flicked through on chilly evenings. That is that the French Resistance was centred around a small café where people passed messages in salami, that singing Russian princesses were Britain's only links with the great Monte Carlo bombings, and that the war lasted fifteen years longer in Australia than it did anywhere else. You may think I'm exaggerating. I'm not. If Trivial Pursuit had not become fashionable when it did, I would still not have heard of Mussolini.

History has got to be the most oddly-taught subject there is. Hopping over the pages of different periods in no apparent order, I've covered Christiaan Barnard, cavemen, the French Revolution, the plagues, Christopher Columbus, the great bull of Knossos and the Battle of Jenkins' Ear, but I'd be hard pressed to list them in chronological order.

What was Henry the Eighth doing during the Agricultural Revolution, and which wife was he doing it with?

You must see the problem. Aside from the hundreds of

events that I will never know about (I only pick World War Two because it seems the most important), the way in which the handful I have covered slot together, or rather don't, is extremely confusing. One thing seems to bear no relation to the next and although the point of learning History would seem, most logically, to be to discover why the world is the way it is today, arriving at that conclusion is practically impossible.

Geography is the same way. Food in Guyana, mining in Wales, population density in Luxembourg, somehow do not merge together to form a picture of the world as a whole, and I can't be the only one who can never find anything on a map except Italy because it's shaped like a boot and Sicily because it's on the end of it. If there's room on the geographical syllabus, I would love to know how to get across London by tube, or from Cricklewood to Poole with three friends and a tenner between us.

The one thing it seems that I have picked up in the way that I was intended to pick it up, is sport.

I'm rotten at it.

Appalling.

Couldn't be worse.

Which is, it seems, the way I'm supposed to be. A genteel English girl in the 1980s is clearly not earmarked for a great sporting career.

Look at Wimbledon. Why is it that England is unable to produce any world-shattering tennis players? I mean, here I am, slap bang in the middle of my education, tennis lessons every week, what is it that isn't being pumped into me that's being pumped into kids my age in West Germany and Sweden? Must be something.

Tennis isn't really a sport in England, it's a courtly pastime. In terms of significance, I suspect that the winning of sets ranks rather lower than the thinness of the cucumber in the sandwiches and only marginally higher than the colour of the piping on the tennis whites. Tennis is about what to do at summer parties in between glasses of Pimms.

Especially if you're a girl. If you're a boy, the standard of your tennis is nearly as important as the standard of your legs, but if you're a girl then taking tennis seriously is *just not done*. The thing to do is giggle and shake your fluffy tennis skirt as you lose by a drastic amount and then disappear into the marquee for a drink. Taking it seriously does about as much for femininity as embroidery does for masculinity. People automatically make assumptions about your muscles, your politics, your attitude to the opposite sex . . .

I think they should introduce a prize for the best losers at Wimbledon. We could have a champion team of girls who trooped quickly on and off the court ('Love-sixteen! Oh sorry, is it meant to be fifteen?') and then danced gaily around the pavilion afterwards pouring orange juice and sugaring strawberries.

Think how that would confuse the opponents of competitive sport! All those poor kids that *win* the egg-and-spoon race every time and never get the loser's cup.

The new trend in non-competitive sport just proves the point that we are a non-sporting nation. Now it seems that a desire to excel at sport must be positively squelched by sports teachers around the country. How daft.

Suits me, I mean, I'm a sporting failure. When winter comes, bringing with it the lacrosse stick to be oiled, the other − better − players to be avoided, and the inevitable encounter with the hard, cold ground, I'm the first one at the teacher's desk with a packet of cough sweets and a note that my mother never wrote. Those who enjoy the challenge of a snowy field scattered with weapon-wielding opponents can play for as many school teams as they like. I've never felt that it's *me* who's losing out when I am tucked up in my coat on a comfortable bench, cheering occasionally for my team as they stumble painfully about the pitch – quite the reverse. After all, everybody has their area in which to shine and why should those whose talents lie in sport rather than other fields be denied the right to display them?

Yet now, from some obscure sense of protection towards the unathletic young, some state schools are cutting down on (or abandoning altogether) competitive sport. It's mad. Children are just as competitive as adults, if not more so. The sports field is the safest and easiest place for them to burn up any excess competitive spirit – let those who want to fight it out do so on the pitch. Meanwhile, the rest of us are content to relax with our cups of coffee and watch them at it.

So might I suggest, if there really is going to be a national curriculum, that history and geography are given a face-lift and music and sport are kept up for those who can do it, but optional for those who can't. It's hardly fair or sensible to allow musicians to show off their talent, but ban talented sportsmen from competing.

After all, can we sing at Wimbledon?

10 Busy Doing Nothing

The Problem of What to Do in the Hols

My life is structured around holidays. Minor ones, such as lunch hours, evenings and weekends, and the major month/two month ones. I spend most of my time watching the clock, waiting for my little break or full unconditional release (end of term).

After a week or so of sleep, of course, one has to begin thinking about how to milk the full enjoyment out of the holiday. Usually this is achieved by spending the next three weeks asleep. Let the unconscious work on the problem. Nowadays, unfortunately, as I am nearly seventeen and must face up to responsibility in life, I tend to have enough work to fill several holidays. Translations, essays, vocab learning, reading, reading, reading . . . (not that I don't like reading, but an exhausted person can only take so much Ulysses on a sunny morning). The prospect doesn't make you leap out of bed.

One way of getting myself out of bed at weekends and during the holidays is by playing tennis. I like it, but unfortunately all my local friends are too lazy to join me so I find myself having lessons with the tennis coach instead.

As I have mentioned before, I am not your talented sporting all-rounder. Steffi Graf does not put her insomnia down to me. I can get the ball over the net — but this seems to be more of a negative thing than anything else, since it appears that my obsession with 'Getting It In' is hampering my chances of cultivating a stylish swing.

The tennis coach is a jolly interesting chap. It's all in the mind, apparently, and we spend most of the time finding images and mental exercises to help me along. The only problem with that is that, as you may have gleaned, I am not an unselfconscious person, and I do feel a tad rough around the edges at this particular tennis club.

'Think of a smooth action as you play the forehand,' suggested my tennis coach. Mine was swimming under-water — silly idea, since I was going to have to act it out, but it was too late to change it.

'An interesting choice,' mused Mr A. 'One lady I tried this on imagined that she was stroking her mink coat.'

I felt suitably humble.

'Another girl thought of brushing her horse,' he added thoughtfully.

Sometimes he waxes mathematical, which is not at all my sort of thing. I do not perhaps take it as seriously as I might if I understood anything about it. I remember one day when he described how important it was that the ball passed the net at the correct angle.

'I'm talking ballistics here,' he said.

'No no,' I said, 'You're making a lot of sense.'

A lot of the principles of these tennis lessons seem allegorical for other areas of my life, probably because I have them very early in the morning after a night of hard drinking. But I tend to relate various factors to other things. My coach thinks I'm a very negative person generally, due to the fact that, when asked to score my grace/talent/ability on a scale of one to ten I always give myself twos and threes. I think this is more to do with a phobia I have of giving myself a jubilant 'Ten!' for grace and being met with an amused raising of the eyebrows from him. Not that he'd do that – the more positive you are the better he likes it – but I harbour these hang-ups.

I get a lot of pep talks during the hour-long sessions. Every so often he calls me up to the net and gives me some image, or talking-to which I imagine as I stand there will have a magical Professor Higgins-type effect and suddenly the right mental string will be plucked and I WILL BE ABLE TO PLAY. I race back to the centre of the court, pulsating with renewed vigour and enthusiasm, and miss the ball completely.

So anyway, I have these tennis lessons early in the morning to get me off to a good start during the holidays. My parents will only give me a hard time if I don't. They like me to have tennis lessons. There are a few set parental phrases which always come into play during the break from school:

If you lie in bed all morning, you waste the best part of the day.

Should you be reading Jackie Collins?

Why don't you start revising for your exams?

I'm sure Grandma and Grandpa would love a visit.

Well, if you need money that badly, I hear Monsieur André is looking for a shampoo girl.

Why not get in touch with Julia – you were great friends in primary school.

It's only a very short run up to A-levels you know.

How long is it since you did any guitar practice?

Mrs McDonald tells me Alice is spending the holidays doing a project on Ancient Rome.

You may not have set work, but you can always READ AROUND your subjects.

Your wardrobe could do with a good clear-out.

It's about time you learned how to cook.

Don't just lie there.

Talk to me in Italian, I'd love to hear how you're getting along.

The car needs washing.

Your hair needs washing.

I thought you watched this *Neighbours* at lunch-time.

When I was your age . . .

But you only saw her yesterday!

And just when did Mrs Brigstocke say you all worked too hard?

Look, we've got that Linguaphone, you might as well use it.

When are you going back?

At least it's better now than when I was little. They used to try and get me interested in the daftest things – like gardening. My parents love to garden in the summer. They can get back to Mother Earth like I suppose they did in the seventies – dress in brown flares and Wellingtons and kneel in the flower bed pulling things up. Sometimes they bring things home in little pots and plant them. Then they come trekking into the house for a cup of tea as the light is fading, tired, aching, muddy-trousered but triumphant. In the winter – hell, let it grow.

When I was small I got quite into all this activity. I had my own little plot which proffered one or two wrinkled, off-pink radishes like baby gerbils every year. I believe I grew two small marigolds in 1981. I couldn't take the weeding, though; I always pulled up the wrong things and, besides, it was boring. I liked the bit where I stood up, hands in the small of my back, and looked (lazily but happily) down on my small crops. The parents could do everything else.

These days I still have my own little plot: to be out of the house any time when gardening is being done. It took a long time for me to get these nails, you know; I haven't forgotten the days when, every Friday night after my bath, I would plead desperately with my nanny to let me grow at least one nail long, for making daisy chains, and then had to stand there and watch her hack all ten off with her vicious round-edged scissors. Now I'm allowed to have them properly, you don't think I'm about to get them all broken and full of mud, do you? Any contribution I make to the garden is purely a decorative one, like lying in a deck-chair.

I prefer to spend my days doing something more intellectually stimulating, like shopping. Shopping's a well good laugh – or it should be.

It's practically impossible for even an innocent fresh-faced sixteen-year-old like myself, whose greatest crime is pretending she got on at Baker Street instead of Finchley Road, to buy anything in a shop without feeling like a fugitive from Holloway.

If I'm shopping alone, I can just about get away with a bit of browsing (all cameras trained and dogs struggling on the leash). If I go with a friend, however, I can't get into a shop without an army of peachly-painted sales assistants making a human stockade in the doorway and asking sweetly, 'May I help you?'

'May I help you?' is vendor/teenager code for, 'What are you about to steal, dearie?'

If they would only stop bandying code-words and be more direct, one could be more blatantly rude back. It's just the awareness of fluttering hands re-arranging the display next to each one I stop at, the feeling that someone is following me carefully round the shop, that niggles at me. I have only ever shoplifted one thing in my entire life, and that wasn't exactly a video recorder or a mink stole. I have to admit that Jessica and I did come across an open, half-empty box of chocolates on display in the Covent Garden General Store and take one each. Crime didn't pay, for me anyway – it was a Turkish Delight.

And even when they do not make it clear they suspect you of serious shelf-hoovering, shop assistants take great pains to show they do not believe you have any money.

'Can you recommend me a nice brooch for my mother?' asks a nice, normal sixteen-year-old. (Well, actually it was me, but the principle's the same).

'Not in your price range, actually dear,' said the sales lady.

How on earth can they tell what you can afford just like that! Can their super-hi-tech video cameras actually send ultra-violet rays into my wallet? I would have liked to tell the woman that I was, in fact, a Getty, buy the entire shop and give her the sack.

Not that your average teenager *does* have as much money as they would like. Obviously, there is a limit to the amount that parents should give their kids – it's not much better when one person gets a frighteningly large allowance because she'll be the only one that has it so she'll either have no use for it or spend it on other people, which will put her in a bit of a difficult position.

But there is a problem there. We are at school during the week and have homework at the weekends, so we don't have time to work. And yet, at this sort of age, we need more money than we have done before. Sure, we can still go out for hamburgers etc. which don't cost much, but there's only a certain number of special occasions that you want to celebrate in an unflatteringly-lit menuless fast food bar where the food is wrapped in wax paper and dumped unceremoniously on a plastic tray by a person in a silly hat and a manic grin. A proper meal out would be nice just once in a while.

And a socially-active girl who doesn't live in a particularly active social spot and cannot really catch the last train if she wants to have any sort of long evening out, is stuck with walking home at two in the morning. Even a mini-cab (which doesn't feel that safe anyway) can be pretty expensive going all the way across London. I think perhaps your parents are meant to pick you up, but I don't know what sort of parents would be prepared to do that on a regular basis. Money is needed in large quantities for even the shortest taxi ride.

In the holidays, of course, you can get a holiday job, and that's what most people do. There's not much choice, of course, it's basically working at a hairdressers, a restaurant or a shop.

You can work in one of the aforementioned hamburger joints – having once perfected the manic grin and the ritual chanting ('Small or regular fries?', 'It's our own brand of cola') – but that will put you off that kind of food for the rest of your life, so the money problem is in fact heightened.

A hairdressers isn't that much more pleasant, since it mainly involves (for the unskilled labourer) a lot of sweeping up of hair and shampooing of scalps. I suppose if you smile a lot and ask people about their holidays and whether they're having their hair done for any special reason then you get a lot of tips, but I wouldn't imagine it's much of a laugh.

But then, I've never had a job. I'm far too lazy, I'd much rather just sacrifice my social life. Or out-guilt my parents till they make a donation. Champagne socialism, thy name is Victoria.

There is one aspect of the holidays that we haven't yet discussed, of course, and that is GOING AWAY. Going away on holiday provides a wonderful opportunity for the observing of parents, siblings and other problems.

The first holiday that I can remember is one in Dorset

with my family when I was two. All I really remember is one horrific night when my brother – then aged five, annoyed by the sound of me sucking my dummy in the dark, yanked it out of my mouth and threw it behind the wardrobe. It rather struck the keynote for our relationship in the future.

My parents rushed to the scene of the crime and spent several hours vainly trying to move the enormous wardrobe, followed by a concentrated period of time trying to convince me that it was about time I threw that last remnant of childhood away anyway. That night I became a woman.

Probably as a result of that, the next few holidays were with Other Families. We would take a house somewhere with family friends for a month or so – hopefully one with children about our ages. There was one particular family which we holidayed with two or three times. I was about four, yet I remember experiencing very complex emotions, centred mainly around my serious crush on the son of the family. I didn't think he could tell and I remember resolving that, when I was older and rich, famous and beautiful (one out of four ain't bad) I would reveal to the world that this chap had been my first love – upon which he would realise his terrible mistake but it would all be too late. And you think your four-year-old is just worrying about whether it'll be getting jam for its tea. We also started a small nudist colony, I remember, and thought the adults were all very uptight for refusing to join in.

After a few years of that, we reverted to a normal hotel, just the four of us, each year. The only problem with that for us children was, we weren't with people our own age. I was a little young for Giles to spend all his time with – I remember passing one holiday getting blissfully in the way of what might otherwise have been a rather nice little holiday romance for him. Then he started wanting to go on holiday separately from us and, for about two or three years running, I just gave him a massive tear-riddled guilt trip on the floor of his room until he agreed to come after all.

Last year, it was finally the end for Giles. He abandoned us mercilessly and bought a cheap package to Tunisia with his girlfriend. I was a bit stuck because, having resolutely told my parents that there was no way I was going on holiday with them alone, I found myself facing the guilt trip that I had always given my brother – if I didn't go then they couldn't go, and why should I ruin everybody else's holiday for my own selfish gains . . .

So, martyr-like, I instructed my father to fit a French plug to my typewriter ('I can always sit in the room and write a novel') and agreed to go. (Note: I'm sorry if that phrasing offends anybody, I remember coming back from that holiday and writing a similar thing in *the Telegraph* and getting a rather stern letter telling me that I should not 'instruct' my father to do anything; I clearly treated him as subservient which was terribly wrong. You do not, I thought, know my father. If anyone *does* take that to mean I treat my father as subservient then please don't worry unduly – I value my life).

It is, I know, appallingly ungrateful and wrong to be anything other than thrilled at the prospect of any holiday, and jolly mean to suggest that being alone with my parents would not be a joy and a privilege – but what do I really have in common with them? One or two chromosomes. Would you go abroad with a couple twenty (!) years older than you, who share totally different friends, hobbies and beliefs to you? And my parents are great – I'd certainly rather go away with them than anyone else's parents – but somehow, faced with the prospect of two weeks in an empty-but-of-geriatrics hotel, I was slightly underwhelmed.

Turned out all right in the end, of course – you knew it would, didn't you? There were a few young people at the hotel, including a rather nice German bloke that I got to know quite well. "Klaus" was a real only child (as opposed to my temporary state) so I saw how lucky I actually was.

Besides, I didn't argue with my parents anything like as much as I had expected to. They turned out to be really quite easy-going. Of course, the moment we got back to London and couldn't push the door through the pile of post before the burglar alarm went off, found the goldfish dead and the milk off, that holiday mood slipped somewhat, but it was good for two weeks.

Especially since from now on I will probably be holidaying with my own friends. A girl can't spend all her time with her parents, you know, it's too inhibiting. I have to admit that holidays aren't going to be nearly as luxurious on my own – it'll be rat-infested youth hostels and no food, not nice coastal hotels and own bathroom. Maybe I *should* . . . but no, no, one holiday alone with parents is enough for me.

Two begins to look like carelessness.

11 Getting the Breaks

Problems at Christmas and other Festivals

For everything there is a season. In Britain, of course, few things occur in the seasons they are supposed to.

What could be more depressing than, two days after you have danced jubilantly out of the school gates for a month's holiday, to walk past W. H. Smiths and see huge 'Back To School!' signs glaring out at you? Well, perhaps having your house hit by a freak flash of lightning, killing your family and burning all your possessions, could be more depressing – but not much. W. H. Smiths must hate school-children. I spend most of my holidays worrying that I have not yet bought a new geometry set for the coming term. (Now I'm only doing English, French and Italian, but I still feel guilty if I do not buy at least one geometry set per term). It always seems too, that just as we start back for the new school year in the autumn, out come the tempting autumn packages of TV programmes, just waiting to lure a girl from her vocab learning. Not that TV packages are as tempting as they were when I was young, back in the early eighties. What do you get nowadays but a lot of 'vintage comedy' (Terry and June for the fortieth time) and 'intense drama' (pretty superficial, but they swear a lot)?

Easter eggs go on sale several months before Easter so that when the festival itself rolls around you think the very sight of another Creme-anything would kill you.

Summer holidays are flogged all through January, just to rub in how very unpleasant it is to sit in front of the blow heater on a snowy Wednesday morning as you alternatively burn your knees, freeze your back and scorch your favourite jumper trying to heat it on the light bulb.

Christmas, of course, wins them all. The king of overfloggedness.

I made the catastrophic mistake, in about 1983, of sending off for a catalogue – ONE catalogue – before Christmas. Ever since then, around September each year, hundreds of the little blighters jam the front door with ideas for Christmas presents, Christmas wrapping, Christmas decorations. Some of them go for the large-scale allure 'Open this envelope NOW – you may have won a luscious Mercedes 190', or, even more blatantly, 'You have been CHOSEN to take part in our GRAND DRAW, your name will enter the LOTTERY BONANZA as soon as you send off your order worth £900 or more!!!!'

You get the soft-porn ones. 'Why not send off for this satin-look camisole-and-knickers set, big enough for two, with handy trapdoor!', 'Send off today and receive FREE hernia belt for the man in your life.'

Possibly the most boring ones of all are the young-parents' brochures, advertising all sorts of toys so that kids can Play-As-They-Learn. I can just imagine the little toddler ripping open its blackboard kit and thinking, 'Bloody hell, I wanted that sub-machine gun from Toys Toys Toys'.

The best way is to check out what the friends' parents are buying and go one better. I remember the Christmas I got a Sindy house that had one more room than a friend

of mine's did. I really milked that as far as it would go –
'Gosh, your poor old Sindy looks a bit cramped in there.',
'I think Barbie will entertain Ken in the second drawing
room – oh, sorry, you don't have one, do you? No don't
feel bad.'

The thing is, having leafed through these blasted cata-
logues since September, by about October you do start
feeling guilty, and in November you can't relax until everything is bought. This feeling is certainly not weakened by
the Christmas decorations that are just EVERYWHERE by
October the third.

What we need is a good action group, an animal-liber-
ation-front type of organisation, a Christmas Rights
assembly who would watch out for any premature cel-
ebration. Any early decorations would be taken down in
the night, untimely Christmas cards burned, precipitate
streetlights cut down. Then, from perhaps December the
first, shops and people would be allowed to start decorating.
It would be pretty good to go out on Dec One and find
everything suddenly transformed. So if there is any funny
business of that nature this year, you'll know who's to
blame . . .

I do still absolutely adore Christmas when it does get
here however. I am perfectly prepared to admit that I am
totally uncool and unwicked, I can be unmitigatedly thrilled
by fairs, games, Disney films and Christmases – my childhood is not over yet.

Funnily enough, my Christmases are better now than
they were when I was younger. Not when I was *really*
small, obviously when I was five or six (hardly there at all)
Christmas was amazing, but it went through a bit of an
anticlimactic phase between the ages of eight and eleven.
Buying the presents was good (when I was very little, my
nanny bought my presents for me, and didn't tell me what
they were because I couldn't keep a secret), and the prep-

arations were fun, but the day itself never quite lived up to it. There was just us and a couple of grandparents for lunch – purple party hats worn rather out of tradition than enthusiasm, and it showed – every year one grandparent would say, 'This turkey's nice and moist, dear. It was a bit dry last year' – like Bruce Forsyth's weekly joke.

After lunch I would rush to the TV in time for the end titles of the Christmas *Top of the Pops* which I desperately wanted to see. The grandparents would fall asleep for an hour, then leap up with cries of, 'What's for tea?', while we tried to jump-start toys that came with No Batteries Included.

Then, suddenly, it cheered up again. It started when we tried Christmas lunch with the neighbours (that is to say, the people who lived next door, not a travel agent style of saying we went to Australia for the holidays) and last year we actually had guests from somewhere else, they DROVE to our house, like any normal lunch engagement. It turns out that we're not the only family who found Christmas was not quite like the Yardley perfume ads.

People always say that when there are little children about at Christmas, you experience the real magic. Unless something very bizarre happens in the growing up process (apart from stopping liking horror films and starting liking spinach), then I can't believe that is true. I have never experienced anything but the true grue (as in 'some') of the festive season when little children are about, to pull things off the Christmas tree, refuse to shut up and watch the Keith Harris and Orville Christmas special that's meant to keep them quiet, run about in my room reading my diaries, trying to play the guitar, seeing which of my new Christmas presents bounce, sampling my make-up (ALWAYS using lipstick as blusher) etc. etc. Perhaps that *is* the true magic of Christmas, and I'm just seeing it through Scrooge-coloured glasses.

I think Christmas is better if you just have (rather than real children) teenagers who behave like children (might I recommend myself). Of course you know that teenagers' status fluctuates constantly. According to my parents, I want to be an adult when it comes to staying out late but a child when it comes to being driven to places. As I see it, I am expected to be an adult when it comes to helping in the house but a child when it comes to Talking To My Parents Like That and Showing A Little More Respect. At Christmas, everyone behaves like a child so its okay. I strongly believe that a sixteen-year-old and a nineteen-year-old are just the right age for stockings and advent calendars and every so often I decide to believe in Father Christmas. That's not so easy, of course, when he's tramping through a Boots commercial suggesting present ideas, but otherwise it's possible.

Which brings me back to my original point about the Outside World spoiling Christmas. I don't go with the flow of criticism about commercialisation from a religious point of view – I think if Christmas is a religious time for you then you should be able to withstand a few cartoon reindeer in the shop windows without your faith being tried, one has little to do with the other. It's just when it all happens too early that it's annoying.

As a matter of fact, I don't think there's nearly enough commercialisation in the modern world. Take the card industry. Load of layabouts. Alright, they invented Fathers' Day so you feel guilty if you don't take him a cold boiled egg and a Hallmark card on June the eighteenth, now they think they can just rest on their laurels. Well I have news for them – there are plenty more occasions which are as yet underdeveloped.

Passion Sunday, for example. Do you know when that is? I thought not. Why should that not be a national holiday, with passion-fruit stalls in the street, Terms of Endearment on in the evening, general heightening of national passion? Answer me that.

Lady Day and Quarter Day coincide. Who takes advantage of that extraordinary lunar occurrence? We should all be out there, drinking White Ladies and eating Quarter-Pounders.

Palm Sunday. Will *you* be getting your palm read? Will *you* be buying a potted palm for That Special Person? Will *you*, in fact, be whipping out a couple of surprise tickets for Palm Beach? I bet you'll find the answer is no.

Then there's Low Sunday. Speaking as a particularly low person, I do not appreciate being overlooked.

What were you doing on, say, May the eighth 1988? It was, by the way, Rogation Sunday. You should have been out Rogating merrily, throwing Rogation parties and Rogate-crashing other peoples'. You can make up for it this November, perhaps, by celebrating the birthday of Guru Nanak Dev Ji.

But do you see my point? All these opportunities to spend money, make money, buy cards, buy presents, sell, sell, sell, and we're letting it slip through our fingers! Pull yourselves together, British Industry – these are not holidays, you know!

12 | Call Girl

Problems on the Phone

When I was a child, the telephone was not an official toy. It was supposed to be serious.

Of course, I treated it like a toy. I used to get together with a few schoolfriends and phone shops etc. which we knew to have answering machines – then leave silly messages. You can imagine the sort of thing. For some reason, ice cream shops were popular butts:

'Hello, I'd like to leave a message for the strawberry ice cream. This is a cone speaking. I'm sorry I've been so depressed lately, but my girlfriend has been a wafer so long.'

Well, we thought it was hilarious.

There were the real practical-jokey ones – leaving a message on several travel agents' answer phones telling them to send hundreds of brochures to any girl we didn't particularly like. I think the idea was that she and her family would be tempted to move away from the area, or some such thing.

As we grew up, we graduated to the live phoning. There were the old favourites ('Hello, is Mr Wall there? What, no Walls at all? How does your house stand up then?') About as funny as a Physics test on a Monday morning.

Some of them have been around for a good while; when my father was little, he apparently used to find people in the directory named Smellie, and call up to ask, 'Are you Smellie?' And this from a humorist.

Then there was the phoning of the sex shops pretending to be a little old lady, the heavy breathing, the bomb threats . . . (well, I have never actually tried the latter, although on double-geography days I have been sorely tempted).

But now, it seems, all this is to be encouraged. There is a whole world of exciting telephone services available to the bored child at home. There are horoscopes, music lines, interview tapes – the spectrum is infinite. (If that image is impossible, put it down to bomb threats during Physics lessons).

I can't imagine that it's very much fun. The naughtiness, the clandestinity was all I was revelling in when I phoned Rubber City and 32 Flavours. I have to admit that I have tried calling one or two of the available services nowadays (strictly in the line of research, you understand), but most of the time it seems that I get through to completely the wrong service.

One tempting advert (Find Romance This Christmas, 0898. . . .) led cryptically to advice for Capricorns. An interview with Bros turned out to be, in fact, Mr Frustrated's Angry Line. Some of them are preceded by a brief outline of the cost involved, and one or two of the adverts say 'We would advise consulting your parents before dialling' in extremely small print, but it's not too hard to understand how parents are finding enormous telephone bills arriving out of the blue when they thought their kid was sitting quietly in his room playing with his Transformers.

Perhaps the most inexcusable of all are the Party-On-The-Phone lines. Now they are nasty. The original Chatline (six or seven people are all connected to the same line and, apparently, have a conversation) closed down – I think it was banned – but a crop of fresh beguiling spores have sprung up to replace it. The adverts are cunningly placed in teen magazines, usually structured around a highly good-looking boy and girl chatting seductively down the wire, a strong temptation for lonely kids on a Saturday evening. The reality is rather different. Not that I, you understand, would EVER sit at home on a Saturday evening for ANY reason other than I was completely tired from a hot date the night before. I must have called during the day, while ill, or something like that.

Anyway, what tends to happen is that several people shout, 'Hello! hello?' for a few minutes, then a little conversation is struck up: 'Where do you come from?' (It's *always* Battersea), 'What do you look like?', 'Are you black or white?', after which someone hangs up or you get cut off. I don't know about these new lines, but on Chatline there was a monitor who used to cut in every so often and say, 'There are three of you on the line' and if only two have been talking . . . well, just think about it for a minute.

The only fun I ever extracted from this strange experience was a little gentle exercise of my vocal skills. I used to use different accents, names, details etc. and just try to create characters for myself to see if I could carry them through. The only thing was, they weren't very toughly tested on Chatline. The most interesting was once when I put on my South African accent and spent ten minutes defending Apartheid. It's interesting how far you can go before people realise that their legs might be being very gently pulled.

There was a very brief service to help teenagers with crushes on their teachers. There are plenty of Agony Aunt lines, but this was a special sideline. I only know because I read about it, but I was never able to get through, which is a shame because it sounded fascinating. What on earth could an Agony Aunt possibly have said?

Perhaps I am unsympathetic to the feelings that my peers harbour for their teachers. I am on slightly sticky ground here since I do have a slight crush on one of the teachers at my school. I'd better not say whom, but I think everyone knows except for Him. Everyone else has a crush on him too. I do mean to be more sophisticated about it, but it doesn't really work. I remember spending an English lesson telling the whole class, teacher included, about how amazing he is. No doubt my English teacher scuttled straight to the staff room and told him all about it.

This is all because it's not a real thing. I know it's a crush. It's not as though I want to go out with him or anything daft like that, although I wouldn't mind having his children. But really it's not serious – really! I don't know what it would be like to be properly in love with a teacher, perhaps some people think an Agony Aunt would come in handy in a situation like that. But surely there are only two options – tell the teacher in question about your feelings and let him/her take it from there, or stifle it. I think you would have to be a good few bricks short of a load not to see those options and work out which is the more sensible.

I do know a couple of people who have had affairs with teachers – not at my school, you understand – and I have tried to find out how you go about getting it started. Apparently, you begin by borrowing books from them and suggesting times to meet and discuss them. Ever since hearing that, I have been very embarrassed about borrowing books from teachers – which is annoying, as it's something I often want to do for purely innocent reasons. (I remember being very enthusiastic about a book that my English teacher, Cathy, lent me – no doubt she will now begin to suspect me of ulterior motives. Well, maybe she won't, since she knows about my Other Crush).

Anyway, after borrowing the books, you're supposed to stumble across them at a party (the teacher, not the books) and get into a deep conversation. Then they drive you home. The likelihood of me bumping into one of my teachers at a party is about the same as the chances of meeting John the Baptist there. My teachers all go to Glyndebourne, or the pubs in Hammersmith. Very few of them drop into your average Cricklewood get-together.

So I have little use for the Agony Aunt, but I could've tried out my South African on her I suppose. No doubt I am not the only one who likes using these lines for role-playing. There is probably a whole sub-culture of Scotsmen, Cockneys and South Africans who don't really exist except on these lines where they are all too busy trying to stop their own complicated dialect from lapsing into Welsh to notice that everyone else is faking it too.

Why do I choose a South African, I wonder? Is it just completely at random? Freud would have had a field day. If he was around today, he'd probably have his own line.

13 | Down the Tube

The Problem of the Declining Standard of TV

I used to watch a lot of TV. I still remember particularly good little sequences of TV timetabling – on a holiday morning, for example, it used to run: *The Monkees, Champion the Wonder Horse, Zorro, Why Don't You?*

Not that I actually ever liked *Why Don't You?*, I just watched it. It was that hypnotic title sequence in which you were invited to switch the TV off and go and do something else. Got me glued every time. It had (has? I think it's still on) a very cliquey feel about it – here's eight kids from Glasgow having a wicked time, sort of thing. It always annoyed me that there was a huge mob of them, yet they could never think of anything more exciting to do than make a barrage balloon out of matchsticks and watch a film about someone who collected spoons. It was a good idea to put on a programme suggesting things for kids to do, but if you didn't have access to seven friends and infinite rolls of sticky-backed plastic, you couldn't take part.

Champion the Wonder Horse deserved several awards though. It was brilliant. Despite it appearing that there were only ever about four episodes. Every time I watched it, it

seemed to involve the horse overhearing two evil men planning to turn an old woman off her property because it had
an oil well underneath it. The horse would tell the dog,
who would tell little Ricky, who would tell the Sheriff, but
not be believed, until the end when the horse would be
patted, given a carrot and told that it could join the police
force any time.

The Monkees was also a classic. I can't remember anything about any of their plots – the plot never seemed to
matter, just as long as there was an opportunity to stop
and sing 'Daydream Believer' somewhere in the middle.

Saturday nights were well timetabled too: *Nanny, The
Two Ronnies, Dallas, Mastermind*. That was in the days
when *Dallas* was really good, and I had the phone picked
up and was ready to discuss the week's episode with my
friends the second Philip Capice's name flashed across the
screen. It was before the producers suddenly realised that
young people were what was wanted and they didn't have
any, so they started causing horrible accidents and bringing
younger actors in to play the same parts. It was before they
cottoned on that they were looking homely next to *Dynasty*
and had to bring in hallucinogenic dreams and assassination
plots in Martinique. Those were the days. JR had only
been shot once: now he's been got so many times, I worry
everytime he has a Bourbon-and-Branch that it will spurt
out of the holes.

What about English soaps? Americans still produce the
proper luxurious, frothy kind of soap. In England we seem
to be going for the gritty exfoliating kind.

Take *Eastenders*. In order to re-create realism, there
seems to be some sort of contract clause about personal
attractiveness. I've never seen such an ugly bunch of characters in my life. I'm a teenager – if I want to see excess
weight and zits, I can look in the mirror. Besides, who
wants a social message twice a week? Every episode some-

one's getting done for drunk driving, or fiddling taxes, or being told they've got AIDS when we know they've been sleeping around. The thinly-veiled moral warnings are slipped in liberally, and it gets annoying after a while.

And everyone's so gloomy and grey. Whenever a happy spell breaks out, you know it's only a matter of time before someone's cat gets run over or they find themselves in debt.

They could take a leaf out of *Neighbours'* book. A symphony of pink-and-purple happiness, a world of barbies and No Worries where no problem takes longer than three days to solve.

Of course, *Neighbours* is very 'in' at the moment. It struck just the right chord at the right time – it has just the atmosphere you want to sink into after a grim school day, and it only takes twenty minutes so there's no time to get bored and you don't neglect your homework. (Well you do, but not because of *Neighbours*). It's so universally watched that it's now a unit of measurement, like Christmas. ('When shall I phone?', 'Oh, after *Neighbours*'.) Sometimes you don't even have to mention the name. ('Shall we go for lunch early and be back in time, or go at two o'clock?')

My father likes to point out all the signs of cheap trashiness in *Neighbours*; he won't accept that that's part of its charm. So the Ramsays' house, give or take a few flower arrangements, is suspiciously similar to the Robinsons', the Mangels' and the Clarks'. So nobody goes anywhere for lunch but the Coffee Shop, and when they say, 'Let's have a night on the town', they mean, 'Let's go to the Water Hole'. So the actors are still out of breath from their dash from one soap set to another – tearing off their *Young Doctors* coats and green *Sullivans'* jumpers and pulling on their orange-and-yellow *Neighbours'* uniforms. So there's no reference to the outside world – every female character has had a bash at being Paul's secretary and the cook in the Coffee Shop, and the only guests at Scott and Charlene's

wedding were the people who lived in their street. So what?
It's how we'd secretly like to live. Who wouldn't enjoy
strolling in through the back door of any house in their
street, knowing that there would be a group of good-looking young people drinking tea and eating biscuits?

It's a fantasy world, what's wrong with that? I'm always
suspicious of people who like realism.

Take *Playschool*. After twenty-five years, it has been
killed off to make room for a '1990's-style show'. *Playschool* was an integral part of my nursery-school days. At
half-past ten, we all congregated in the school hall (the
headmistress's living room – there were only two mistresses)
to watch it. And my nursery school was highly progressive;
girls and boys alike fought over who got to wear the black
velvet dress and push the pram. But for twenty-five minutes
the banging of doors, the throwing-about of Lego bits and
the arguing over the dressing-up cupboard was silenced as
we sat enthralled. We all took part. We sang the songs. We
tried to tell the time from the clock. (Although they only
ever taught you how to tell when it was Something o'clock
and to this day, it's the honest truth, I can't tell anything
else).

I don't know about everyone else, but I got stuck in there
emotionally, not just physically. Remember Humpty? – the
one who was so fat that while prissy little Jemima and
Hamble and boring old Big Ted and Little Ted were having
new clothes fitted, he never got any. He just sat there in his
old green waistcoat and I learned the meaning of empathy.

And the euphoria of guessing which window we were
going to go through was the high part of my week. Even
better than staying up till seven o'clock on my nanny's
night off.

It's sad that children's programmes have to be updated.
It's happening with books too – the new trend in introduc-
ing children to reality at an early age. Instead of Hobbits

and playing-card people, modern children's 'fiction' centres on truancy, street crime, divorce and lead-free petrol. All manner of sexual tendency must be represented to rid the child of prejudice. I can't see how this would make any difference. The child concentrates on what it finds interesting in the book; take parenthood for example. It seems that single parenthood must be well documented in children's books now, because generations are growing up believing wrongly that one mother and one father is the only normal family unit. But do books really influence children? All I read when I was little was *The Famous Five* – Julian, Dick and Anne's parents were never even mentioned. They just hung around with Aunt Fanny on Kirrin Island. I never thought that was odd – I was interested in the children, not the parents. What did I care who else lived in the house?

Representing minority racial groups is another matter – sure, children should be used to seeing different coloured faces around them, and they should be represented. But why should a child be forced to recognise something totally irrelevant to it, like what Mummy and Daddy (or Daddy and Daddy's friend Eric) do after Julian, Dick and Anne have gone to bed? It actually goes against what I believe to be the fundamental principle – what you do when your bedroom door is shut is nobody else's business but your own. Deliberately bringing in a gay father and pointing out that he is normal is trying to stamp out a prejudice that a four-year-old doesn't have. Much better for it just to learn as it gets older that sexual practice, within reason, has little to do with moral worth and character. Why shove gritty realism in a toddler's face?

Anyway, I'm still waiting for this '1990's-style show'. Other pleasant, although obviously highly outdated and unfashionable, children's programmes seem to have remained. Like my favourite, *Rainbow*. I don't know what sort of decade you'd slot that one into, it's pretty bizarre whenever you date it. When I first watched, aged not very much, I didn't understand the principle of glove puppets. I could never understand why Zippy and George always had to stand behind a wall. Even when they went on an outing, to a barn dance for example, they always seemed to pop up behind a bale of hay.

Who on earth thought that up? I mean, look at the set-up: a house containing a man in yellow trousers, a giant bear, a pink effeminate hippo and a strange sandy-coloured thing with a zip for a mouth. Now I don't like too much reality, but this is going a little far, don't you think?

The balance of reality versus fantasy in a child's life seems very peculiar. They are spoken to in a totally different language while they are babies for no reason at all, but then between about four and seven when everything should be fantasy, it's getting more and more realistic. Tiny little boys re-enacting the Vietnam war. Life is weird.

After the *Playschool/Rainbow* years, the major centre of a kid's televisual life is the Saturday morning slot. When I was small it was *The Multi-Coloured Swap Shop*, since when it's been through the *Saturday Superstore, Get Set For Summer, The Magic Picture Show* (or something) and goodness knows what else. Now it's *Going Live!* which is really no different from any of the others. The presenters are essentially all the same type too – they just look different. Like *Dallas*.

I don't know whether this programme (that is, all of these programmes) has got worse, or whether I have just become more critical. Now it seems that they're forever getting things wrong, cutting to things that aren't there, the phones don't connect, the cameras wobble. Like *Dallas*.

I have to say that the best programme on TV at the moment is *The Waltons*. I never miss it. If you want your child to see how it ought to grow up, let it watch that. It's brilliant. Why can't we all go and live on a mountain with Grandma and seven children? They don't need money, everyone is happy and helpful all the time, the parents never shout, the children never cry. Why shouldn't life be like that?

I'm not a realist at heart.

14 | Future Tense

The Ageing Problem

There comes a time in the life of every teenage girl when she has to start thinking about the future. It seems to happen earlier than you might think, probably due to the English system of committing yourself to arts or sciences at school when you're only aged fifteen. It was then that we were invited to think about the university courses (if any) that we wanted to take, and the eventual career that we wanted to follow. It was then that representatives of different professional fields came to tell us what would happen if we Did What They Did. It was then that we panicked.

I am quite lucky, in that I have never been good at very much. I saw the brilliant kids struggling with their choices, courted equally by the languages and mathematical departments, wanted equally by everybody. I did not have that problem.

'I've been thinking about doing History A-level', I would say to my History teacher, to be answered with a panic-stricken look and a lecture on how much work there was involved. I remember having to leave a Chemistry lesson early for my meeting with the careers advisor.

'Perhaps I'll say I want to do Chemistry,' I said as I left

the room. I could still hear them laughing when I got to the interview.

Since I was two-and-a-half, when I decided I wanted to be a writer, my ambitions haven't changed very much. I have been through phases of considering advertising, English teaching, even Law, but nothing that involved major changes to school courses. My poor mother still, I think, harbours a secret dream of my becoming a stockbroker, but I somehow doubt that will ever be fulfilled. Giving me a maths text book was like some sort of Desmond Morris experiment – everyone laughed and clapped when I held it the right way up.

Of course part of me really wants to be an actress. Isn't it the same for everyone? My school has made every attempt to thwart me in this, it seems, since every time there is a school play on when I am not in an exam year, it's a musical. (See section on school for attempt to describe my singing voice). This year, for the first time, there is a non-musical. Do I get the chance to demonstrate my acting skill with a strong emotive part? I'm playing a bloody soldier. This goes against all my principles, but an aspiring actress must put these aside. Also, I doubt my performance will do much to further the cause of war.

Whose bright idea was it to make me a soldier? For a start, I'm going to look ridiculous, especially since the girls playing women are of the tall willowy variety. I'm going to look like a pepper pot with a pony tail. Plus, I absolutely cannot speak in a deep voice. The best I can do is a sort of thirteen-year-old-boy-with-voice-breaking, and then only with both eyebrows clenched and my chin tucked into my chest. I'll be far too busy concentrating on keeping this up, breathing in (no doubt some kind of uncomfortable restrictive undergarment will be coming into play) and walking with a manly stride to try and give anything like a reasonable performance. Little chance of Martin Scorcese happening by and making me a star.

So forget the idea of being an actress. Besides, I get no encouragement from anyone on that score. Whenever I mention it, people start banging on about pantomimes in the North and your children not recognising you. I don't know how I'm planning to slot any kind of career around seven of them.

My romantic picture of myself as a writer, thundering away on an old manual typewriter, my hair held back with a biro, while the children play happily around my feet, strikes me as somehow unrealistic. I wouldn't dare suggest at my frontier-breaking school that I plan to stay at home with children anyway. I would probably have my mouth washed out with soap and my fingers chopped off. No self-respecting eighties woman harbours desires like that. I'm one of the few people there not taking Economics in preparation for a career in the city. Most of them already have their briefcases initialled in gold, and their pinstripe suits laid out on the bed.

Don't get me wrong, I'm certainly not an anti-feminist, I love to see women striding out there, calculator in hand, but I am also warmed by the idea of a pile of fresh snowy laundry, a larder stocked with homemade jam and seven well-brought-up children. Of course, the idea of a pile of muddy, grass-stained laundry, a mound of unwashed saucepans and seven noisy children running riot and refusing to sit down and watch Children's TV fills me with horror, so I will no doubt get over this housewifely bent. But I don't think there's a ruthless career woman in me battling to get out. We shall see.

Besides, it is now too late for me to be a doctor, a mathematician, musician, statistician, historian, businesswoman, geographer, scientist, artist, marine biologist, classicist, butcher, baker or candlestick maker, because I have now chosen my A-levels and I am committed. Or I should be.

English, French and Italian, I seem to be doing. Not, I think, what my parents would have chosen for me. Languages, says my mother who can speak four or five of them, can be easily picked up later on (Easily picked up! Ha! Two miserable sodding years of German and I know three words) whereas *real* subjects, maths and so on, must be learned in school.

But the same nagging old fashioned voice in me that finds housewifery somehow appealing, also sees 'being educated' as knowing several languages, and being able to paint and play the piano. I read a lot of Jane Austen. When it comes to painting and playing the piano, you might say that if I had one arm and a disease which attacks the visual and aural senses, my ability could not lessen. So I'm concentrating on the languages. Italian and French because I saw them referred to once as the Romance Languages.

The only problem is (here comes a warning for all fifteen-year-olds about to choose their A-levels) I am learning nothing about the world at large. I'm reading in three languages, but at the moment the *material* I'm reading is against a background of the Industrial Revolution, *le Terreur qui suivait la Révolution Française* and ... well, I'm still learning the basic grammar in Italian but no doubt something historical will pop up soon enough. I will probably never now know what the world looks like and who says what. Whenever they give us model essays on general subjects, they're always full of, 'As Napoleon discovered ...' and, 'a similar idea was upheld in the fourteenth century ...' So, anyone with any similar choice offered to them, be warned that three languages and an aspiration to learn more about the world you live in go together like chocolate and Branston pickle.

I suppose I'm looking forward to getting older, there

must be *some* laughs in store. (??) I'd like to say I was looking forward to getting married (presumptuous, but I hope I will). Unfortunately, it's not really the case. It doesn't seem to be possible to stay happily married to one person for your whole life. 99 per cent of husbands are unfaithful, I read somewhere the other day. What a depressing thought. The husband in *The Waltons* is never unfaithful. True, there aren't any other women in the programme except the two old ladies that live on the hill, but it's the idea that counts. Still, who could be excited at the prospect of seeing someone they'd been married to for thirty years? For goodness' sake, I meet someone I would like to go out with about once a year, imagine trying to find someone you wanted to marry. And I don't want to get married unless I think I'll be in love with that person for the rest of my life – which doesn't seem to be possible. Watching TV is so depressing, EVERY-ONE has an unhappy marriage. Except the Waltons.

It must be so boring to be married, anyway. No flicker of excitement when you bump into someone you're attracted to (or if there is, you're not allowed to do anything about it). So you stop going to parties and things because there's no point if you just have to walk around with your husband and try and find friends you both like – half as likely as on your own. Even little things you take so much for granted, like having a friend over to stay the night and just talking till it's light – well, you can't do that when you're married, can you? *He* has to be there the whole time, no wonder people get bored with each other.

Then the timing is all wrong. When you're thirty, you're (one would hope) still interested in your husband so you want to spend time with him, but maybe you've got small children so you want to spend time with them, but then again, you're just getting ahead in your career so you have to concentrate on that.

Then you're sixty, you retire, but your children have left

home and you're stuck with him – Mr Boring, whose views on everything you've heard a million times over.

But come to think of it, who'd want children anyway? Yeah, I say I want lots, but that's only theoretical. Who really wants a pack of little brats that find you irritating, and tell their friends about you, and never help in the house, and shout at you, and think they have more right to everything than you? Parents must be mad.

It's so much nicer surely being *young* and having an infinite world of other young people to meet, and all the men are unattached, and your biggest problem is having to go to school which is really pretty brilliant because you secretly like everyone and enjoy the basic set-up. Wonderful, blissful experiences like going to the caff when you should be in a lesson, and cracking up during a very serious lecture or a prayer and getting a nasty look from the teacher in front . . . I mean, it's so normal now but it'll be over soon. The relationships you can have, when your friends are your confidantes, and the people with whom you spend most of your time, and who think like you do, and know exactly when you feel like skipping assembly, or a hug, or a cigarette.

They say that when you're young all you have is problems and fits of depression. Well, obviously there are a few, or life would just be boring, but there aren't *that* many. Of course, so far I've only tried being young – maybe when I'm older I'll look back (like everyone seems to) and say, 'Goodness me, who'd be young again, all those problems and hassles?'

It's probably unavoidable. But let me just record now, and someone can remind me of it when I'm old and cynical, that, so far, life has been pretty wicked.